AF580737

I Didn't Do It

Also by Elle Gonzalez Rose

The Girl You Know

I Didn't Do It

ELLE GONZALEZ ROSE

BLOOMSBURY
NEW YORK LONDON OXFORD NEW DELHI SYDNEY

BLOOMSBURY YA
Bloomsbury Publishing Inc., part of Bloomsbury Publishing Plc
1359 Broadway, New York, NY 10018
50 Bedford Square, London, WC1B 3DP, UK
Bloomsbury Publishing Ireland Limited, 29 Earlsfort Terrace, Dublin 2, D02 AY28, Ireland

First published in the United States of America in July 2026 by Bloomsbury YA

Bloomsbury books may be purchased for business or promotional use.
For information on bulk purchases please contact Macmillan Corporate and Premium Sales Department at specialmarkets@macmillan.com

Library of Congress Cataloging-in-Publication Data
Names: Rose, Elle Gonzalez author
Title: I didn't do it / by Elle Gonzalez Rose.
Other titles: I did not do it
Description: New York : Bloomsbury, 2026.
Summary: High schooler Dina, the daughter of a confessed murderer, thinks her luck has changed when Kai, the new popular boy, invites her to a cabin getaway, but when people start dying, she quickly becomes the primary suspect and must prove her innocence.
Identifiers: LCCN 2026012846 (print) | LCCN 2026012847 (e-book)
ISBN 978-1-5476-1848-4 (hardcover) • ISBN 978-1-5476-1849-1 (e-book)
Subjects: CYAC: Murder | Family problems | High schools | Schools | Mystery and detective stories | LCGFT: Thrillers (Fiction) | Novels
Classification: LCC PZ7.1.R66927 Iad 2026 (print) | LCC PZ7.1.R66927 (e-book)
LC record available at https://lccn.loc.gov/2026012846

Book design by Jeanette Levy
Typesetting by Six Red Marbles India
Printed in the United States at Lakeside Book Company
2 4 6 8 10 9 7 5 3 1

To find out more about our authors and books visit www.bloomsbury.com and sign up for our newsletters.
For product safety–related questions contact productsafety@bloomsbury.com.

For Paul, who I've been urgently trying to contact.
Please check your Letterboxd

AUTHOR'S NOTE

Please note that this book contains depictions of murder, a parent in the prison system, blood, violence, and parental emotional abuse as well as references to suicide and bullying and past homophobia and transphobia.

I Didn't Do It

EXHIBIT A: POLICE INTERVIEW TRANSCRIPT

RA: Good morning, Miss Soto. You feeling okay? Need some water? Tea? Tissues?

DS: M'fine.

RA: You need anything you let me know, all right?

[no verbal response]

RA: Well, my name is Detective Ron Aydin. I'll be leading the investigation into what happened to your friends. I just have a couple of questions for you.

DS: I already talked to someone.

RA: I'll be taking over the case from the officer you spoke with at the scene. I just want to get a clearer picture of what happened. Dig a little deeper into the original report. Looks like the first person that was identified was . . . Kai Thompson. Wanna start with telling me what happened to him?

[no verbal response]

RA: All right. How about his sister . . . Kiki. Care to tell me more about her?

[no verbal response]

RA: Listen, Dina, I'm not the enemy here. I'm just trying to figure out the facts so we can get you home, all right? Don't you want to go home?

[nearly five minutes of silence]

RA: You have to know this isn't looking good for you. Cabin soaked in blood. Bodies all over the place. Only girl left standing is the daughter of a convicted murderer. The headlines are gonna be writing themselves, unless—

DS: *[inaudible response]*

RA: What was that?

DS: I didn't do it.

1

I'm a better liar than you'd think just by looking at me. Everyone in my family is.

I don't *like* having to lie, but sometimes it's worth it. Like now, as I run my finger along the skirt of my dress, the fabric soft and delicate as a cloud. I can't find it in me to regret what I had to do to get it. Not yet.

When we first saw it at the mall, Mami had eyed the neckline warily, shaking her head when I lingered in front of the shop window for too long.

"Too much," was all she muttered under her breath before tugging me toward the secondhand store to search for new pants for my little brother, Mikey. New clothes—*really* new—have never been an option, and especially not now. Mami often tells me how grateful I should be that we're the same size so we can share. Pants. Blouses. Even shoes. But it's hard to find silver linings when you wake up to half your closet missing because your mom didn't do her laundry again.

After that, the dress was all I could think about. How I'd look in it. What it would be like to wear something clean and fresh and new with no patched holes or permanent stains. How it would feel to have something that was truly and completely mine.

Thoughts of ripping the dress off the hanger and hurrying away as fast as I could had come in frequent flashes. I'd thought trying it on would shake the bug out of my system, that once it was on, I'd see it wasn't as perfect as it seemed in my daydreams. Scratchy against my sensitive skin or too loose where it should've hugged my meager curves.

But it was just as perfect in reality as it was in my fantasies. Soft, crepelike fabric. The perfect shade of olive green to bring out the barely noticeable glow of my skin. Molded to my body like it was custom made to my measurements.

No one would blame you for taking it, I told myself as I shoved the dress into my backpack before I could talk myself out of it. *You deserve good things too.*

Guess I'm pretty good at lying to myself, too.

All I could hear was my heartbeat as I crept out of the dressing room, weaving between the other girls and their friends and mothers and boyfriends as quickly as I could. I didn't let myself breathe until I made it to the bus stop. Kept looking over my shoulder all the way home, waiting for someone to come screaming at me to stop.

Every night I opened my bag and looked at the dress, just to convince myself it was real. That I'd actually done what I'd spent so many nights dreaming about. That the dress was mine. I hadn't thought twice when Mami asked me what I was smiling about at dinner that night, replying, "I got an A on a test." So fast my brain hadn't even registered that it was a lie, responding like I would to any of her other prying questions. Maybe that's what makes us such good liars—we're able to convince ourselves it's the truth.

This morning, part of me still hoped I would wake up to find a wrapped box sitting on the kitchen table—the dress perfectly folded between layers of tissue paper and tied up with a ribbon—but the table was empty. Not a note from Mami or a card with a generic message or even the bills we always leave scattered around the house. No acknowledgment that today was different from any of the others.

But I can make it different.

After smoothing the few wrinkles out of the dress, I pull my hair forward over my shoulder, my dark brown hair soft and wavy thanks to the braid I just unwound. Even hours later my scalp still aches from the way Mami tugged my hair into submission this morning, weaving the braid together as quickly as she could before rushing out the door without a goodbye. Beyond the bathroom door I can hear the buzz of voices slowly gathering in the cafeteria for dinner. And, finally, him. His voice. *That laugh.*

You don't hear laughs like that often, not here at least. Sunny Hills Assisted Living isn't as cheerful as its name promises. The residents are quiet, the building even quieter. My first week volunteering here over the summer, three days passed before I heard something that wasn't *The Price Is Right* on the TV in the community room. It was a boisterous thunderbolt of a laugh. Loud and carefree and joyous. From the moment I heard it, my fingers frozen around a dented bedpan, I knew it was him.

Kai Thompson. The new boy at school with the charming smile. Who cracked jokes at lunch like he was holding court and was voted homecoming king without even campaigning.

Peeking through the supply room doorway, I saw him. Curled up next to his grandma, Mrs. Thompson, on her bed, leaning on her shoulder while they scrolled through TikTok on her iPad.

"You're more addicted than me," he'd teased her, earning him a nudge in the ribs that made him giggle.

Something about this place has always made him feel even more beautiful—so vibrant and alive in a place that feels determined to drain the last dregs of life its residents have left. The only reason I'm still volunteering here is because it's the only chance I have to get out of the house. Though, to be honest, I'm lucky they let me stay at all. After everything.

After Papi.

The trial was over a year ago and most of the residents don't remember it, or at least not the details. The ones who do remember—who recognize me—have kept their distance, mumbling under their breath about letting girls like me into a place like this. The murderer's daughter.

But none of the staff have said anything—not to my face anyway. They need all the help they can get, and I'm free labor.

I didn't stay just because of Kai, though. Residents like Mrs. Thompson make the after-school volunteer shifts worth it. She either didn't know about Papi or didn't care—always welcoming me to her room to try out the empanadas her daughter-in-law had just dropped off or asking me to fix the Wi-Fi on her iPad again even though I told her all she needs to do is switch it on and off. I don't mind, though. I'd gladly trade a dozen favors for one of her stories.

In this life Mrs. Thompson was an accountant, but in another one she must've been an actress or a storyteller. Some kind of performer. She has a way of capturing your attention, making you want to sit and listen to her for hours. Stories about growing up as a young Black girl in the South during the civil rights movement, about raising three kids under five alone after her husband was killed in a factory accident, about watching her grandchildren grow into the people she always knew they could be. Kai inherited that from her—charisma like gravity. But he's never needed to tell stories to pull me in.

"Hey," Kai had called out that afternoon when I first spotted him at Sunny Hills, before I could hide in the supply closet, hoping he wouldn't catch me staring. "You're Dina, right?"

"You know each other?" Mrs. Thompson asked, looking between the two of us.

"We were in the same Spanish class last year, right?" Kai asked with a raised brow.

"Y-yeah," I replied, still hidden behind the half-open door.

I'd spent an entire semester lingering on the details of his profile from the last row of Ms. Martinez's Spanish class. The full curve of his lips, the slope of his nose, the way his eyes crinkled when he smiled.

Sitting in the back row made my life easier. If you're in the back, no one can gawk at you, not bothering to keep their voice to a whisper because they know you won't turn around and shut them up. Being in the back made studying him easier, too. I could watch him laugh and joke and tease his friends as the hour ticked by without notice. No one ever turned around. Especially not to see me.

But maybe he had.

"You taking AP Spanish this year?" he continued.

I nodded quickly, worried my voice might crack.

"Guess I'll see you there," he said with a wink I was sure I'd imagined before turning back to Mrs. Thompson's iPad.

I brushed it off as good manners. A boy raised right by his grandma—who played nice, even with girls like me. A girl the world doesn't owe any kindness.

Summer came and went and that moment with Kai started

to feel more and more like a daydream the closer we got to the school year. The first day of junior year, I kept my expectations low and head down. The way I have since the trial, and even before, if I'm honest.

But then he sat down beside me.

"Qué pensaste?" he asked, gesturing to the weathered copy of *Don Quixote* we had to read half of over break, following the "SPANISH ONLY" rule written on the board.

My heart hammered so loud I was sure he could hear it. Glancing over my shoulder, I double-checked that he wasn't talking to someone else. When I turned back to face him, his eyes were bright as stars, a smile tugging at his lips.

"Estaba bien," I replied, using what little confidence I had in me to keep my voice from trembling. "Un poco aburrido."

"Muy aburrido," he replied, rolling his eyes and slapping his own copy onto his desk with a *thunk*.

His accent was stilted, but it had that natural lilt only people who spoke the language at home—heard it from native tongues—could capture. So much like my own that it felt impossible. Spanish had always felt like such a private thing in our family. Reserved for when Mami whispered warnings under her breath at the grocery store, the post office, the mall—the few public spaces we can't avoid—to stay close or look the other way. A language spoken by billions, that somehow felt like it was made just for us.

And now, him.

Every morning after, I braced myself for him not to turn around. But every day he did, offering a smile or a bite of his breakfast sandwich or a story about how he fell off his longboard that morning, with the scrapes and bruises to prove it. He came around Sunny Hills more often, too. Spent more time with Mrs. Thompson, wheeling her around the facility as if he were a Formula One driver, ignoring her protests as he whizzed her down the hall to the cafeteria. Soon he was coming to visit her every Tuesday and Sunday—the same days I was volunteering.

The Thompsons may have moved to town three months after Papi's trial was over, but ours isn't the kind of story a town this small forgets. He would have learned about me within weeks, if not days. Who my family is. What my dad did. Most people avoided us, and in the few forced interactions I've had since the trial, disgust and distrust simmer just beneath the surface. But that's never been the case with Kai. He's the only person I can talk to who doesn't feel like they're just waiting to run away. The only person who actually seems interested in *me*.

Still, every day I wait for him to turn his back on me like the rest of the world has.

Hopefully today isn't that day.

"Dina!" Arlene, resident director of Sunny Hills, barks at me as soon as I step out of the bathroom. Out of the corner of my eye I spot Kai bent beside his grandma, helping her pull open the tab on her pudding cup. "Are you bringing that gauze over or not?"

One reason I would've left by now if it weren't for Kai and the sweeter residents: Arlene, who acts like I should be grateful to her for showing me basic human decency and not totally shunning me. I almost wish she'd treat me like the rest of the world does. At least then I wouldn't have to deal with her.

I pry my attention away from Kai and grab a packet of gauze from the supply closet down the hall, then rush back. The last thing I need is Arlene more pissed than she usually is.

"Did you mop the cafeteria?" she asks once I've handed off the gauze.

"Not yet," I reply, already grabbing the mop and bucket beside her before she can scold me for not finishing the job sooner.

I stick to the corners, mopping the faded beige tile until my reflection slowly comes into view. It feels pointless, polishing something so worn with years of baked-in grime, but that doesn't matter to Arlene. Half the tasks she gives me are just to keep me busy. The other half are things she doesn't want to bother doing herself.

"New dress?" a voice calls out from behind me.

The rapid *badum badum badum* of my heart echoes in my ears as I whip around to face Kai, my hair smacking me in the face and clinging to the clear gloss I'd applied in the bathroom.

"Birthday gift from my mom," I say, because I can't tell him the truth, and the lie comes out as smooth as it had to Mami.

"When's your birthday?" Kai asks with a smile, leaning up against the pillar beside him.

I duck my head sheepishly, cheeks warm as I mumble, "Today."

Kai's eyes widen. "Why didn't you say anything?" he teases, knocking his fist against my shoulder—goose bumps blooming along my bare arm. "The cafeteria's still open for a few more minutes. Let me buy you a cupcake."

He's already walking backward toward the food counter, pointing his thumb over his shoulder, and it takes more strength than I anticipated to shake my head. I'm already on thin ice with Arlene—blowing off her orders to go eat dessert with Kai won't do me any favors. "It's okay," I reassure him.

His smile drops into a dramatic pout. "You sure?" He sighs

when I nod, letting his arms fall limply at his sides. He walks back over to me slowly, digging his hands into the pockets of his jeans.

"Well, your mom has good taste," he says, eyeing the bodice of my dress with a smile. "Green's your color. Makes your eyes pop."

When Kai's gaze meets mine, all sounds fall away—the distant hum of the TV, the clack of the receptionist's keyboard, the scratch of canes and walkers on the cracked tile. There's nothing left in the world but him, his smile, and the way I look in the reflection of his eyes. Soft and sweet and beautiful—a version of myself I never thought I could be. I resist the urge to lean in, to pull him by the collar of his jacket and do all the things I've been told I shouldn't want. Press my lips to his, run my fingers down the smooth plane of his arms, hold him tight until he can feel the rhythm of my heartbeat—a song written for him.

I swear he leans in closer, not afraid to cross that line. The smell of him—soap and spiced cologne—surrounds me like fog. I'm not sure what he'll do but I'm ready for all of it, bracing myself for something I know I should regret but won't.

"Kai!" Mrs. Thompson shouts, popping our bubble. "Quit flirtin' and help me back to my room."

The pounding in my ears is so loud I don't hear what Kai shouts back, my limbs heavy as I sink back down to the ground, not realizing that I'd leaned up onto my tiptoes. I'm not as good at resisting as I thought.

"Sorry, Good Grandson Duty calls," Kai says, rubbing the back of his neck with a shy smile. He heads back toward his grandma while I collapse onto the column he'd been leaning against. I whip back to attention when he turns around, trying to wipe the lovestruck grin off my face as he calls out, "Were you planning on going to the Halloween dance next Friday? I can make it up to you then. Buy you a belated spooky birthday cookie or something."

"O-oh." My fingers curl into fists, nails digging into the smooth flesh of my palms. "I'm not sure yet. I'll . . ." I trail off, unsure what I'm willing to promise.

Deep in my gut, I know the answer is no—that Mami won't let me. The only reason I'm able to volunteer at Sunny Hills is because I convinced her it would give my college applications a boost, even though we both know college is the kind of expense we'd never be able to afford. Still, we like to hold on to some of our old dreams. All the things that once felt possible.

I'd have a job if anyone was willing to hire me. We've never said it out loud, but I know we're all praying that by the time I graduate next year people will have forgotten about us. About Papi. That businesses will be willing to have a Soto at their register or stocking their back room without attracting the wrong kind of attention. We're lucky Mami was able to find a job bagging groceries at a Costco two towns over, but we know we can't count on lightning to strike twice.

Until things change, Mami insists we stay close to home. She's always been protective, even before Papi's trial. Even before we lost my older brother, Joel. What was once just her holding us close now felt like a vise grip—harsh and suffocating. I'm lucky to have Sunny Hills. If I didn't, I'd only ever be allowed to leave for the essentials. Groceries. School. Doctors' appointments.

A Halloween dance is not essential.

"I'll find out tonight," I manage to choke out, wondering if I've made a mistake.

But I know I haven't when he gives me that radiant smile again, so bright it feels like the best kind of blinding. He backs away slowly, eyes fixed on mine as he holds up his linked fingers. "Fingers crossed."

I whip around, hoping to catch a glimpse of him wheeling Mrs. Thompson toward the elevator in the mirror mounted on the wall behind me, but he's already out of view. All I can see is a girl in an olive-green dress patterned with daisies. Rosy cheeks and soft brown curls. Glossy lips tugged into a smile she didn't think she still had in her. A girl I wouldn't have recognized.

I run my hand along the neckline of the dress again, down the hollow of my throat until my heartbeat thrums beneath my fingertips. Finally, I feel something close to happiness. Finally, I feel beautiful. Finally, I feel hopeful for something sweet and good and pure. Finally, I have a shot at something that I don't have to steal for it to be mine.

And I don't regret a thing.

EXHIBIT B: EXCERPT FROM THE *MILLCREEK SUN*

BELOVED HIGH SCHOOL SOCCER COACH SENTENCED TO LIFE IN PRISON

The "trial of the year," as declared by social media, has come to a shocking and abrupt end this afternoon. Following a bombshell confession midway through his trial for the murders of students Jose Perez and Danny Bauer, former Millcreek High soccer coach David Soto has been sentenced to life in prison.

The trial took the country by storm after popular true crime content creator *Crime and Dine with Hailey Winters* posted a video covering the case. At the time of this publication, Winters's video has garnered over five million views. Livestreams of the court proceedings amassed audiences of over a hundred thousand viewers per day, the comments flooded with debates over whether Soto was guilty. But with his Friday-night confession, Soto put an end to any and all speculation, much to the shock of not just viewers following along, but the victims' families as well.

"If there's one good thing to come out of all of this, it's that that monster is where he belongs," Jose Perez's mother, Sonia Perez, said exclusively to the *Millcreek Sun* following the sentencing. Her son, a Millcreek High senior, had been coached by Soto since he first joined the team his freshman year. "I hope that man never sees the light of day again. It's the least my son deserves."

Soto's family had been outspoken about his presumed innocence but were singing a different tune at the sentencing Tuesday morning. "We pray for his soul every night," Soto's wife, stay-at-home mother Emilia Diaz Soto, said in a statement on behalf of the family. "All we can ask for is peace and privacy as we try to move forward."

David Soto will be eligible for parole in 2058, when he's 72 years old.

2

Daydreams carry me through the rest of my volunteer shift. Add bounce to my step as I walk to the bus stop. Keep my grin in place the entire forty-five-minute ride home. I don't need music when I can lose myself in dreams of a night with Kai. Dancing and laughing and maybe more. A night like the ones on the telenovelas Joel and I used to watch after dinner every night. The type of night I didn't think was possible outside of a screen.

But my dream shatters when I see our garage.

MONSTER, painted in the color of the devil himself. Paint drips down from each letter, staining our driveway like a pool of blood. There's a halfhearted swipe through the *M*. Either Mami or my younger brother, Mikey, must've seen it and tried cleaning it off before giving up and heading inside.

It's not the first time something like this has happened, or even the worst. The first few weeks after Papi was arrested, it was constant. Words painted on every surface of our house. Sometimes the car. LIAR, DEVIL, MURDERER. Notes slipped beneath the front door, calling us even worse. Rotten fruit and bricks lobbed at our windows as we told ourselves to be grateful they never aimed for our heads. It didn't matter that their real target—Papi—wasn't home and would never be coming back. We were still the faces on the news, holding back tears as we stood alone on his side of the courtroom. We had his last name. Me and Mikey had his face—his deep brown eyes and thick, boxy brows. That was enough.

Before I even get into the house, I know things won't be pretty. They haven't been for months. From the dishes piled in the sink to the smell of rot leaking from the fridge. But I'm still startled by the sound of Mami in the kitchen chopping furiously, pulling apart a rotisserie chicken like it's to blame for vandalizing the garage.

"Set the table," she orders after I close the front door behind me, not even looking up from the cutting board.

I know better than to protest or take too long. Quickly, I toss my bag beneath the desk in my room and carefully place the chair in front of it. The chances that Mami would go through my bag and find the rumpled dress are low—especially when she's this upset—but it wouldn't be the first time she's gone through my stuff. None of us have ever done anything worth hiding, even before Papi was arrested. But that's never stopped her suspicions from running wild—accusing us of running off to be with friends she told us to avoid, or hanging out after school with people she's deemed "the wrong crowd." Worrying about things we've never actually done matters less now that she has bills and rent to worry about.

With my bag safely hidden, I roll up the sleeves of the sweater and jeans I changed into after my shift and grab plates and cutlery from the kitchen cabinets. It feels silly to still set the table when there's only three of us. Half the time Mikey doesn't even finish his meals. He'd rather push his food around, making faces out of mashed potatoes and peas, than eat, but I can't blame him. These days I barely have any appetite either.

Papi always insisted on "proper" dinners together at the table. Before his parents passed, it was something they'd insisted on too—something he carried with him through several foster homes and, finally, with us. He called it a sacred part of the day. A chance to unwind with family, to appreciate each other and the food Mami spent that afternoon preparing. Now it's usually cold McDonald's fries and silence. We still leave Papi's and Joel's seats free. Set plates down in front of their chairs like they'll be coming through the door any minute.

That's another thing we're not willing to let go of yet. Coming together as a family. Pretending we're not broken.

Mami calls out to Mikey, and he trudges into the room, rubbing the sleep from his eyes. A year's gone by since Papi's trial and Mikey hasn't gotten a solid night of sleep since. He hasn't been able to shake the nightmares that started right after Papi's arrest. I dealt with them then, too. It was so soon after we lost Joel, and too much for our minds and hearts to handle. Back-to-back tragedies, but the world only cares about one.

We'd do more about Mikey—the lack of sleep and appetite, the slip in his grades, the notes he's bringing home from his teachers about fights and failed tests—if there was more we could do. Mami's job bagging groceries barely covers the rent as it is. There's no room in the budget for tutors or doctor's visits. With the amount of detentions he's been landing for picking fights with kids who can't keep their thoughts to themselves, we're bound to face the consequences of ignoring Mikey's problems soon enough. For now, though, that's another thing we're pretending hasn't changed.

Starting your first year of high school is already tough.

It was on me, and that was before Papi's reputation followed us wherever we went. But I was lucky—I had Joel. Two shy kids who could spend their lunches dreaming of the people we could become someday, far away from home. We were each other's only friend, but just knowing there was someone in my corner made the maze of hallways and people less intimidating.

I wish I could be that for Mikey—the beacon of hope in a complicated world of cliques and gossip and endless pressure. I hoped by the time he started at Millcreek High the student body would've moved on to the latest piece of gossip, but in a town this small you don't easily forget a crime this huge. We don't have to do or say anything for people to want to take us down. Sticking together means drawing attention. Drawing attention means welcoming trouble. We're better off on our own—another way this town has torn our family apart.

For now, all Mikey can do is learn to ignore the monsters that visit him in his dreams—the way I did.

The stack of bills is back on the dining table. I make sure to swipe them before setting the table, tucking them into a drawer in the living room for now. We can't keep ignoring the bright red warnings and past due notices, but keeping the lights on and food in the fridge is more important right now than paying back the lawyers with the too-wide smiles. We let ourselves fall for the confidence in their voices once—when we trusted that they could bring Papi home—but we know better now than to believe anything they say. Including their deadlines.

We sit down and pick at our food wordlessly. I'm used to the sound of knives and forks against plates, quiet grunts and sighs as we eat before cleaning up and heading to bed for another sleepless night. Today the silence weighs on my chest like a thousand bricks. My breath catches at every new sound.

I practically jump out of my seat whenever Mami so much as looks my way, panicking that she'll find a way to read my thoughts. That the question I haven't asked yet is written all over me.

That, somehow, she *knows*.

"You look sick," she says without looking up from her chicken. Mikey gives me a confused look, but I don't need eye contact to know the statement was meant for me.

"Long day," I say quickly, hoping she won't notice the waver in my voice. "I think I ate something weird at lunch."

If Mami suspects anything about me or my answer, she doesn't let it show. The silence settles in as we turn back to our food. Mami never asks about our days anymore, and we never ask about hers. Asking means opening the wounds of the outside world. The dirty looks and whispers sent Mami's way by customers. The shoves and taunts Mikey fought off between classes. All the gaps in our lives without Papi and Joel that we're still discovering.

Our days aren't worth dwelling on. All we can do is move forward.

The question sits on the tip of my tongue as Mami finishes the last of her food, slipping closer to the surface with each strip of chicken that disappears from her plate.

Just ask, *just ask*, *just ask*, I repeat to myself, hoping that eventually it'll stick. Worst-case scenario, I don't go to the Halloween dance like I assumed I wouldn't. I'll get a lecture from Mami about spending time with the "people we can't trust" and the importance of staying close to home, and that'll be that. The same spiel we've been getting for years, even before Papi's trial, about why we can't go to sleepovers or birthday parties for our classmates—because the world is a dark and cruel place, now more than ever. And the only people we can trust are each other.

Best-case scenario, Mami's feeling generous—maybe remembers it's my birthday—and I get to go. My gift: one night where I can pretend the past year never happened.

"There's a—"

"Fill the bucket in the pantry with warm water when you're done," Mami says, cutting off my question before I can ask it. Swiftly, she takes her and Mikey's plates and scrapes the leftovers into the trash. "We should clean the garage before morning."

All the courage I'd worked up leaks out of me like a balloon, leaving me deflated and slumped in my seat. I'm too caught up in my disrupted plan for her request to sink in. Water. The garage. *Monster.*

My arms ache at the thought of scrubbing the garage clean. Red paint doesn't wash off without leaving a stain—they always make sure of that. It'll take at least an hour to wipe it down to a pink smudge. Another to cover it back up with the white paint we bought in bulk from Home Depot. Mikey and I exchange an exasperated look. With cleaning and catching up on homework afterward, it'll be close to midnight by the time we get to bed.

It doesn't make sense to paint the garage now, when the sun is already well past set and we'll need streetlamps and flashlights to see what we're doing, but we've done this enough times to know Mami doesn't care about the garage itself. It's about not letting people see what the world thinks of us. If we work late into the night, the paint will be gone by morning and no one will remember that we were branded as monsters the night before. It doesn't matter that we already know what they think of us. Or that nothing we do will change their minds.

"If we leave it up, we let them win," Mami said once, after Mikey complained while we scrubbed the graffitied f-bomb off our front door.

There's no world where we win, though.

Mikey and I know better than to argue. I shovel down the last of my chicken and cold peas from a can. While Mami washes the dishes, we follow orders and fill the bucket with soap and water, lugging it out front together. Mikey whispers my name while I'm grabbing sponges from the bathroom, gesturing for me to come to his room. After making sure Mami is still washing dishes in the kitchen, I cross the hall to his room and carefully close the door behind me.

"Happy birthday," he says as soon as the door clicks shut, pulling a cupcake out from behind his back. A rainbow number nine candle is sticking out of the frosting. "That's the only candle they had," he mumbles apologetically before setting the cupcake down on his desk.

In my panic about asking Mami if I can go to the dance, I'd completely forgotten that today wasn't supposed to be like other days. I'd let the monotony get to me—convince me that this wasn't a day worth celebrating. And who could blame my family for forgetting? Losing a son, then a father a few months later? But Mikey didn't forget.

I don't ask him where he got the cupcake or the candle. The same way I didn't ask him what happened when he came home from school with a split lip last week. I've heard enough through the grapevine to know that he's picked up the wrong kind of habits. Last month the manager at the convenience store down the block told me to tell Mikey he'd call the cops if he came within ten feet of the store again. If Mami looked up long enough to see what's happening, she'd hold him so tight he'd burst. Become even stricter that she already was—which feels impossible. As worried as I am about the path he's going down, I don't have it in me to tell on him. It would just make everything—*him*—worse.

Instead of dwelling on the why and how of the cupcake, I pick it up and hold it beneath my nose. We need to move fast—Mami will come looking for us any minute—so I wrench my eyes shut and think of a wish that feels worthwhile.

I could wish for things to go back to normal, but that won't bring back Joel. Or Papi. And it's not like life then was perfect either. We've always had our flaws. If we didn't, maybe Joel would still be here. It's too late to wish for normal now.

So, I wish for something new. As I blow out the candle, visions of Kai—his smile, his laugh, the way he looks at me—blossom behind my closed eyes. A dream I wish to become reality. A chance to break free. A chance to be myself. A chance to find out who I am outside the four walls of my house, outside of being the daughter of a killer.

As I blow out the candle, I let myself hold on to something foolish: hope.

3

For the first time, I dread seeing Kai. I linger in the doorway of our AP Spanish class, considering faking a stomach bug and camping out in the nurse's office. But then there will be tomorrow, and the next day, and the next, for two years until we graduate. I can't avoid him forever. While the thought of turning him down hurts, I tell myself that the invitation didn't mean as much to him as it did to me. That it was just a gesture of politeness, not something more.

I wasted enough time walking to class that Kai's already at his desk, bent over his notebook with his tongue stuck out in concentration as he sketches a superhero midflight. One of his original characters, he explained to me after I peeked over his shoulder at Sunny Hills this summer.

"I'll start my own MCU someday," he'd said as he flipped through the notebook, enough sketches of heroes in latex and masks fighting monsters among skyscrapers to fill at least three comic books. "The Kai Thompson Universe," he'd added with a flourish as he waved his hand through the air.

Nothing usually breaks Kai's focus when he's working on a sketch. I could be standing next to him banging pots and pans together and he wouldn't look up until he got the final detail exactly how he wants it. It's earned him a couple of good whacks from his grandma. I breathe a sigh of relief as I take my usual seat behind him. With the sketch only half done, he'll probably be working on it until the bell rings and I can put off facing him until tomorrow.

But, of course, I'm not that lucky.

"Hey," he says, breaking out into a wide grin that would normally make the butterflies in my stomach take flight.

"H-hey," I mumble back, gripping my backpack strap so tightly my knuckles go as pale as the notebook page Kai was working on. "The scene's really coming together." I gesture to his sketchpad, still open to the panel he's been working on for the past two weeks. A climatic battle between his still untitled hero and Dr. Osmosis, the big-bad with the ability to conjure typhoons that could destroy entire cities in seconds.

Thankfully, that does the trick. Kai perks as he shifts back around to look at the sketch while I settle down at my desk. "I think the blocking was what was tripping me up. Dr. Osmosis should've entered from the right side of the panel instead of the left, or else that throws off the entire flow of the battle."

He continues on about the physics of their respective powers, and while normally I'd hang on to his every word, I'm trapped in my own spiraling thoughts. Too focused on trying to figure out a way to let him down gently—or avoid the topic of the dance at all—instead of giving him my full attention.

I'm not able to avoid the topic for as long as I'd hoped, though.

"So, you coming to the dance next week?" he asks suddenly, whipping around in his seat and picking up exactly where we left off yesterday.

Staring into his wide, eager eyes hurts more than I thought it would. There's something so soft and earnest about him.

Sincere in a way I didn't think was possible outside of the romance books I used to sneak from the library. With his smooth brown skin, full curved lips, and the glimmering sword earring dangling from his left ear, he's the spitting image of the perfect leading man.

And I'm about to turn him down.

"I . . . can't." Saying it hurts almost as much as watching him process it. His grin slowly melts into a frown, the rosy tint in his cheeks fading as his eyes break away from mine to face the ground.

"Oh. That's cool," he says with a nonchalant shrug and a new, hollow smile.

"I really want to," I add before he can turn back around. "I just have to help my mom with a work thing that night," I explain, the excuse I'd prepared last night.

The lie hits me hard, even though it rolls off my tongue easily. But I can't sit here and let him think that turning him down doesn't feel like plunging a knife straight through my heart.

"Dang, that sucks," he replies with a genuine frown.

"Maybe next time?" I offer, cursing my foolish heart for making more promises I can't keep. There won't be a next time, and based on the look on Kai's face, he knows it.

"Actually . . ." he begins hesitantly, and I brace myself for him to let me down easy. To tell me he's not interested anymore, or that the invitation was a onetime thing.

He looks over both shoulders before turning back to me. When he speaks again his voice is a whisper, a secret just between us.

"My parents have this cabin in the woods up by the river. Me, Kiki, and some of our friends are headed up there after the dance. Just for the weekend. Not to, like, drink or party or anything like that," he says quickly, holding up his hands and shaking his head as if to bat that assumption away. "It'll be chill. Scary movies and s'mores type of vibe."

Somehow, he shifts his entire body closer, the edge of his palm brushing against mine so lightly I'm not sure if it was real or if I imagined it. "You could come, if you want? After you finish the thing with your mom?"

If the thought of going to a dance with Kai made my heart race, the idea of spending a weekend with him makes the entire world spin. I feel so weightless I'm sure I'll float away any second. I've forgotten how to breathe, how to function, how to say anything that isn't a high-pitched squeal. A growing cloud of dread lingers in the corner of my mind, but I force it down like last night's dinner.

"Yeah, totally," I say before I can regret it, or realize what a monumental mistake I've just made.

There's no way I'll get to go. I can admit to myself now that Mami never would've let me go to the dance, and there's no way in hell she'd let me spend an entire weekend away. If she had it her way, we'd never leave the house. Never talk to anyone who isn't each other or her.

Besides that, while the idea of alone time—*real* alone time—with Kai feels intoxicating, I can't pretend that spending a weekend in a secluded cabin with his sister, Kiki, doesn't give me pause.

As far as twins go, Kai and Kiki's similarities end at the physical. Where he's sunshine and kind smiles, she's hard edges and dirty looks. Beautiful and cruel, exactly what you'd expect from a cheerleader. Within weeks of arriving at Millcreek High she was linking pinkies with Carla Gutierrez, cheerleading captain, ruthless queen bee, and former girlfriend of star soccer player Jose Perez. A boy I never spoke to but am linked to forever now because of my family. Needless to say, no one in her elite orbit is a fan of me, Mikey, or anything having to do with us.

Ever since Kiki arrived, she and Carla have ruled the halls with perfectly manicured iron fists. Last week they made a girl from the debate team cry because she'd accidentally sat at their usual lunch table. Even if I didn't have my dad's reputation hanging over me like a black cloud, I'd still avoid Kiki's red-hot gaze. Anyone in her path is bound to be destroyed.

Still, I can't fight the thrill bubbling up inside me, making my hands shake and heart race. A weekend away. With Kai. The only person who's ever made me want to step into the sun. Like the wish I'd made on that cupcake last night could be more than just a dream.

Tomorrow I can panic about what saying yes means. How to either let him down gently or beg Mami for permission. But today, I can bask in the way he looks at me. The way he holds my gaze for just a few more moments before the bell rings and Ms. Martinez calls us to attention.

"I'll text you," he says before finally turning back around.

And if I wasn't weighed down by a dozen other problems, I'd float away then and there.

EXHIBIT C: TEXT MESSAGES BETWEEN KAI THOMPSON AND KIKI THOMPSON

KAI: Heads up I invited someone else to the cabin next weekend
KIKI: omg
KIKI: you ACTUALLY have a friend????
KIKI: stop the presses this is groundbreaking news
KAI: stfu
KIKI: is it that dude from the swim team with the braces?
KIKI: bc he said some weird shit to Carla last week
KIKI: don't really want that vibe around
KAI: Nah, you don't know her
KIKI: HER?????
KAI: Yes, she's a her
KIKI: WHAT HAVE YOU NOT BEEN TELLING ME?????
KIKI: does me being your twin sister mean nothing to you???
KAI: Yes
KIKI: wooooooow you're so fake
KIKI: im telling mom you blamed Snoopy for throwing up on her Louboutins
KAI: Okay fine
KAI: Damn
KAI: It's Dina Soto
KIKI: lmaooooo
KAI: What?
KIKI: stop playing
KAI: I'm not playing.
KIKI: ooooooh he's using punctuation, so scary
KAI: I'm being forreal
KIKI: wait seriously
KAI: Yeah

KIKI: since when do you know her

KAI: We met over the summer at grandma's facility. She volunteers there

KAI: You'd know if you ever visited grandma

KIKI: don't try to guilt trip me

KIKI: you know how Carla feels about Dina

KIKI: about what her dad did to her ex

KAI: She's not her dad.

KAI: And she's really cool and chill, I swear

KAI: I wouldn't invite her if I didn't think she was

KIKI: yeah, we'll see about that

4

Saturday, the two-hour drive up to Suffolk County Prison gives me plenty of time to regret my decision. Half an hour on the road and the radio becomes nothing but garbled static, leaving us with just the sounds of the car clanging along for entertainment. Our car was banged up and rusty when we got it off the used lot ten years ago, and it's only gone downhill from there.

With every passing road sign, I consider telling Mami the truth. About the dance, the cabin, Kai. Every time I open my mouth, a new image appears on the empty stretch of road in front of us. Mami pulling over to shout at me until her throat is hoarse. The car veering off the road from the shock of Mami processing what I just said. A lightning bolt striking the car the second the truth slips out of me. There's no point in asking when there's no possibility that it ends well.

Which leaves me with two options: let Kai down again or sneak out.

The idea of going out without permission feels like less and less of a possibility the longer I linger on it. I'm not the girl who slips out her window in the middle of the night. I'm the kind of girl who knows to keep her head down, smile, and follow the rules. When Mami told me I couldn't go to the mall with the few friends I'd made in middle school, I didn't protest. When she didn't let me go to their birthday and slumber parties, I didn't argue. Staying home was easier—safer, she said. And why wouldn't I believe her?

Now, me avoiding my peers truly is the safest option, not just for me but for all of us. Even if Kai can see the real me, there's no guarantee that the others will. To them, I'm probably nothing but a ticking time bomb.

Mami has always told me I'm not like the other girls in Millcreek—not the type of girl who twirls her hair around boys or parties with her friends. But lately, I'm not sure if that's who I really am or just who she needs me to be.

Still. Sneaking out would break Mami's heart. And I don't know how much more of that she can handle.

As always, the prison is bursting with noise. It's welcome, for once. A distraction from my dangerous thoughts. The reception area is packed with misty-eyed women and crying babies. Every week there are new faces between the ones we've come to recognize. The sister visiting her baby brother who's ten years into a twenty-year sentence for burglary. The single mom struggling to keep her band of toddlers in line as she writes their names on the sign-in sheet, warning them to "be good for Daddy." Sometimes the old faces fade. Gone either because whoever they're visiting is free now, or because they stopped caring.

We'll never be able to stop coming. No matter how much I wish we didn't have to, that Papi would come home with us one day. This will be our lives until the day he dies.

We're able to get through security quickly. By now we've come enough times to have a routine. Baggy cotton clothing like sweatpants and sweatshirts. No underwire bras. Nothing in our pockets, not even loose change. We line up neatly in the waiting area, claiming our usual trio of corner seats as we each wait for our turn. Mami goes first, as always—rocketing out of the room the moment Papi's name is called out by the burly guard at the entrance. There's a new slump in her posture by the time she returns. As if another dozen pounds have been added to her shoulders. She keeps her head down, eyes averted from the two of us as she wipes at her nose with a crumpled tissue and mutters something under her breath about us going ahead. Mikey offers the second slot to me with a subtle jut of his chin. I give him a tight smile before heading in.

The room is a stark, almost blinding white. All it does is draw attention to the cracks in the ceiling and the smudges on the wall. Years of grime that no one's bothered to clean up. The familiar hum of whispered conversations isn't loud enough to drown out my thoughts as I approach the booth on the far end of the room.

"Don't look so excited to see me," Papi teases as soon as I slump into my seat and pick up the banged-up phone on the wall beside me.

I can't help but smile as I toy with the phone's cord. I can feel my cheeks warm as I focus my gaze on a squashed bug on the edge of the table instead of facing Papi. He's always had a way of seeing right through me.

"Something happen?" he asks without missing a beat, proving my point.

Lying has become a regular part of our conversations. Mami always warns us not to tell him about the words painted on our house. The things thrown at our windows. The whispered taunts whenever we linger outside for too long. Things are hard enough for him. We all know how guilty he feels for everything that's happened—we don't need to weigh him down with another burden. Still, there's something different about giving him a plastic smile when I know I'm planning something that would tear Mami apart.

"Something at school?" Papi presses when I don't answer, leaning as close to me as he can without pressing himself up against the glass. Somehow, I can still feel his warmth.

Against my better judgment, I glance up at him. While it sucks coming here, I can't find it in me to turn down the chance to see him. To memorize the lines of his face just in case they start to slip away from my memory.

He's aged a dozen years in the few months he's been here. The gray strands that used to peek at his hairline have taken over, thick and coiled tight like my curls in high summer. His light brown skin is worn, blisters lining his cracked palms. Once the only wrinkles he had were from laughter—lines around his mouth from all the times he let out those big belly laughs that were sometimes funnier than the joke itself. There's a new strength to him, too. In his arms—the muscles tight beneath the sleeves of his faded brown uniform. In his jaw—probably from the twenty pounds he's lost since he got here. It's strange, how much he looks both like the Papi from my memories and a stranger. Prison has made him into the type of man people expect him to be—someone with worn hands and hard edges.

"Things okay with your mother?" he asks, and my stomach tightens. I still don't say anything—just the thought of coming up with an excuse makes my gut churn painfully. Hard as I've tried, I've never been able to pull off lying to Papi. He can tell something is off, though, given the way he sighs. "Go easy on her. You know how hard things have been for her," he says. Making more excuses for her, the way he always does.

Things have been "hard" for Mami since they first met. Him, the golden boy of Millcreek High despite his troubled past, and her, the wallflower who could go an entire school year not speaking more than a dozen words to anyone—a wallflower that began to bloom after they met in the rec room of the group home they were both placed in. They'd only overlapped for a matter of days—him between fosters, her in temporary custody while her mom waited to hear back on a DUI charge. But a matter of days was all it took for them to fall fast and hard.

He loved her endlessly—more than even her own family ever did.

"He was my family," Mami told us a dozen times when we begged her for fairy tales before bed and got their story instead—it was our favorite happily ever after.

While their classmates taunted her for her secondhand dresses and her mother punished her with bruises and burns for daring to take up space in their cramped apartment, Papi saw who she could be when someone treated her like a person instead of an annoyance. Lifted her up instead of punching her down.

He's been protecting her with all his strength ever since.

I know better than to argue with Papi when he's defending Mami, so I stay quiet. I'm sure he'd find a way to justify her forgetting about my birthday. That she's overworked and struggling, or she'll probably remember later, even though we both know she won't.

We hold each other's gaze for what feels like hours. We don't say anything, just look into each other's eyes—mine a perfect mirror of his. Part of me has always been comforted by how much people say we look like. That we have the same nose and eyes and laugh. That I inherited his kind soul and easy smile.

As hard as it might be now, I don't think I'll ever regret all the things that tie me to him. That I've inherited all his best parts.

Something shifts in his expression, and for a moment I wonder if he's going to finally, *finally* break down like I've been expecting him to ever since they took him away, but instead he leans in with a smile.

"Go get something from the vending machine," he says with his signature mischievous smile, nudging his head toward his outstretched hand.

I glance down and bite back a gasp. Through the slot in the glass between us, he's slipped me a tightly folded stack of dollar bills.

"But—"

He holds up a finger to his lips before I can protest, smirk still in place as he points toward the vending machines lining the opposite wall. Quickly as I can, I pull the money through the slot and shove it into my pocket—making sure none of the guards perched at each end of the room noticed before rushing over to the wall of machines.

The pickings are slim. Two machines are completely empty and the other three are in desperate need of a restock. Nothing new has been added since we started visiting, but then again, most people aren't in the mood for snacks when they're here. I'm not sure how long the snack cakes, candy bars, and chips have been sitting in these machines, but you can't be picky in a place like this. I shove in the crumpled dollars and punch in the numbers for a cinnamon bun clinging to the top row because it's the only thing that looks like it won't get stuck on the way down.

Papi is grinning by the time I make it back to my seat, cinnamon bun clutched tight against my chest. He gestures for me to unwrap it, waiting until I have it sitting open in front of me to pick the phone back up.

"Happy birthday to you . . ." he begins once I've picked my own phone up. It's already uncomfortably hot in the room, but my cheeks go so warm, I'm worried I'll pass out when I realize what he's doing.

As he continues, he amps up the volume. Until he's loud enough to catch the attention of the other groups seated around us. To his right, an inmate with a shaved head and a neck tattoo joins in. Then another, and another. Then an older woman wiping her tears away two rows down from me. Until almost everyone in the room has joined in for a rousing chorus of "Happy Birthday." The guards eye us warily but don't interject. As much as they might try to take it away, happiness isn't off-limits. I can't help but look around in awe as everyone stumbles over themselves when they get to my name, Papi proudly proclaiming "Dina!" for everyone to hear.

So many of the places in my life feel devoid of joy. School. Sunny Hills. Home. Here. But in those few moments when everyone in the room sings "Happy Birthday" to me, I feel it. The blush in my cheeks slowly trickles away. My heart stops pounding. I'm not overwhelmed by the sudden attention or weighed down by my fears. All I feel is that same fleeting happiness as when Kai asked me to the dance. I know it'll be gone soon, but it feels so good to have it for even a moment.

Papi looks incredibly proud of himself when the song comes to a close and several people give me a polite round of applause.

"Happy birthday, mija," he says with the same beaming smile from all the photos we once had on the mantel. The same smile that the media twisted into something wicked. The same smile as mine. "I know I'm a few days late, but . . ." He points to the cinnamon bun and gestures for me to help myself. The first bite is so sweet it should make me wince, but all I can do is grin. The dough is harder than it should be—stale, most likely. But just like the cupcake Mikey gave me, it's perfect. "Hopefully this makes up for it."

"Definitely," I tease, wishing I could nudge my elbow into his ribs like he always did when he teased me.

I wonder if I'll ever be able to touch him again. Ever feel the warmth of his hand on my shoulder or the strength of his arms wrapped around me, twirling me in a circle. It's a sour enough thought to make the sugar in my mouth turn to ash. My smile falters as I shove those thoughts to the back of my mind. That's the kind of thing meant to haunt me in the middle of the night, not now when I should be enjoying my few moments with him.

If Papi notices the shift in my smile, he doesn't comment on it. Instead he props his chin up on his closed fist as I pick at my cinnamon bun. "School been all right?"

I nod stiffly, toying with a hardened piece of glaze as I weigh what to say next. "I think I made a new friend," I finally confess, choosing to play it somewhat safe. Before everything, Papi was my confidant. My safe space. As worried as I am about Mami finding out the truth, I can't resist the urge to tell someone—*him*—a small piece of it.

"Really?" he asks with a raised brow. I'd be offended by how shocked he seems if I wasn't so self-aware. As much as I might've inherited from him, I'm not social like he is. Not able to win people over with my charm and my stories. And Mami's overprotectiveness didn't make things any easier. After Joel, I would've said Papi was my best friend. Now they're both gone.

I nod again, not trusting my voice not to give me away. That doesn't dull Papi's enthusiasm, though. "He invited me to a dance," I finally settle on, hoping I won't regret revealing that my new friend is a boy. Papi always assured me that anything I told him stayed between us. Hopefully that still applies now. "But Mami won't let me go."

Papi softens at the mention of Mami. His smile crumples into a sympathetic frown. He sighs as he droops slightly in his seat, nodding in understanding. "I'm sorry, mija," he mumbles, as if it's his fault.

I shrug sheepishly, wishing I could hold Papi's hand and squeeze. Reassure him without words that I don't blame him for this. For any of it. But I know if I say it out loud, he'll shoot me down, insist that it was his fault. He's still defending Mami even now. After everything.

"Be easy on her, Dina," Papi says again. It's not the first time he's made that plea. Or the tenth. Maybe not even the hundredth. I grit my teeth, resist the urge to protest. Why do I have to be easy on her when she's never been easy on me?

Papi doesn't say anything and neither do I. Anger seethes inside me at the thought of yet another excuse for Mami being so strict. Like it's something we should admire. Like she's doing us a favor holding us so tight—making it so we're afraid of the world. Of strangers. Like we haven't learned anything from Joel.

Guilt swallows that anger whole, drowns it deep, deep, deep to the lowest pit in my stomach. *She just wants to protect you*, I remind myself, but it's Papi's voice ringing in my ears. No one knows better than Mami how hard life can be when you're not protected. All she wants is to keep us safe.

"I know the world isn't kind to you right now," Papi says after what feels like hours, his voice weathered. He looks at me so fiercely it's like he's trying to melt the glass so we can finally hold each other again. "But you deserve good things, Dina." His voice cracks slightly, and a piece of my heart cracks too. Tears sting the corners of my eyes as he slowly swims out of view. Until all I can make out clearly is the sound of his voice. "You deserve a life as beautiful as you are."

My throat, eyes, and head ache as I struggle to hold back my tears. I let out a choked laugh and nod, just to give myself something to do to avoid thinking about the tears, about the way his voice sounds so helpless. Moments like these make it feel impossible that the world sees Papi as a killer. The person who kissed the crown of my head whenever I tripped and fell. The person who makes the best arroz con gandules during the holidays, and always makes sure to set extra aside just for me. The person I didn't realize was my security blanket until he was gone. How could they look into his eyes and see all those horrible things they sprayed on our walls? *Devil. Monster. Murderer.*

Papi is the best person I've ever known. Now all anyone will know him as is a monster.

I nod with more force once my tears are safely at bay. "I know," I mumble as I swipe at my cheeks even though I didn't let any of the tears slip out. Something shifts inside my chest as I inhale sharply and ground myself until my vision is clear and the pressure has subsided from my temples. The fear that haunted me on the drive up here feels like a distant memory. Papi is right. Even though our lives have gone to shit, I still deserve good things.

Starting with the only boy who has ever made me feel seen.

EXHIBIT D: INTERVIEW WITH DAVID SOTO AND LEAD DETECTIVE RON AYDIN, FOLLOWING DINA SOTO'S ARREST

RA: At any point did you suspect that something like this might happen? See any signs during your monthly visits?
DS: Of course not. Those visits are barely twenty minutes, if that. The guards here are always trying to shove them out the door the second they get here . . . I had no idea . . .
RA: Did you think that this was something she was capable of?
DS: You don't understand, I—
RA: It's a yes or no answer, Mr. Soto.
DS: . . . No.
RA: And if you had any inclination that this was something she was capable of, would you have alerted the authorities, or your court-appointed psychiatrist, Ms. . . . Melfi, about those suspicions?
DS: . . .
RA: Mr. Soto?
DS: I'm not sure.

5

On Halloween night, we turn all the lights off. Mami says it's to make sure trick-or-treaters don't come looking for candy. I bite my tongue as we eat dinner in almost pitch-black darkness. There's no point. We all know no one was going to come to our door, lights on or not.

The dark makes it harder to set up my decoy. Even though my bedroom is in the far back of the house, away from the street, I don't dare turn my light on and risk Mami coming in to scold me. I move as quickly and as quietly as I can—shoving clothes into my backpack and into body-shaped lumps beneath my comforter. I don't need to bring much for a weekend away, but I stash anything that I halfway like into my bag anyway. Summer crop tops despite the mid-autumn chill and dresses I've worn only for special occasions—bumping my shins and elbows into the wall every few minutes as I root through my closet and dresser in the dark. I bite back a hiss as I stub my toe against the edge of my bed, eyes wrenched shut and lips pressed tight to keep from crying out. The house is eerily silent, the way it always is now that we're down to a family of three instead of five. Past my closed door I can make out the distant murmur of the TV in Mami's room. The telenovelas we used to watch together, when I thought our closeness was a blessing. What feels like thousands of years ago.

A new text makes me snap back to reality.

Kai Thompson: Just left the dance! Should be at your place in fifteen

The sight of his name in my phone makes my heart leap into my throat. The text itself, though, cranks up the volume on the ticking clock in the back of my mind. I reply quickly, letting him know I'll meet him down at the end of the block. Mami's bedroom windows don't face the street, but there's no point risking getting caught before I can even make it to the curb. We've developed a sixth sense for strangers entering our space. This wouldn't be the first unfamiliar car to idle outside our house. And they've never lingered for good reasons. The last thing I need is to draw any unnecessary attention to Kai.

As soon as I respond, I toss the makeup and perfume I'd grabbed from the drugstore earlier this week into my bag and close it before I can think of something else to bring. Bag packed, I focus on rearranging the clothes shoved beneath my sheets into a more me-shaped lump. I tuck one of my old dolls up against the pillow, letting her pristine braid poke out from beneath the covers—a near perfect match to my own. If anyone looks closely, they'll be able to see right through my decoy, but it could buy me a few extra hours.

While part of me hopes Mami won't notice my absence at all, I know she's not so checked out that I can disappear for two full days. She'll be up at five tomorrow to get ready for her seven a.m. shift, and while we're usually allowed to sleep in on Saturdays, sometimes she'll come barging into my room anyway, insisting on braiding my hair even though I can do it myself or listing off chores for me to tackle while she's gone. Because she knows I won't have plans—she makes sure of that.

Once I'm happy enough with Decoy Dina, I sling my bag over my shoulder, wincing slightly at the unexpected weight, and pull the folded letter from my pocket. It took ten pieces of paper swiped from the printers in the computer lab before I finally settled on a message that didn't make bile crawl up my throat. Simple and to the point. And, hopefully, enough to calm Mami if she finds it.

I'm out with friends. I'll be back on Sunday by dinner.
I promise I'm safe.

I love you.

My gut tells me the letter, no matter how sincere or how much I assure her that I'm all right, won't do anything to stop Mami from giving me hell once I'm home. Still, it's worth a shot. If I don't give her some kind of explanation, I could come home to find my face splashed across missing posters throughout the city. Though, that's assuming the cops would care about the missing Soto girl.

I hold my breath as I perch on my windowsill, craning my neck for the sound of footsteps as I unlatch the window and push it open just enough for me to slide through. There's still nothing but muffled rapid, overdramatic Spanish. I swallow hard, close my eyes, and brace myself for the fall.

"What're you doing?"

It's a miracle I don't go toppling over the edge of the window. Hands pressed against my heart I whip around so quickly a nerve twinges in my neck. Mikey glances over his shoulder to confirm that Mami didn't hear him before quietly shutting the door behind him. Thankfully, he remembered to keep his voice down.

"Dina, what the hell?" he asks, whispering. "Where are you going?"

I bite my lip, unsure if it's worth telling him the truth. I hadn't planned to tell him anything because I didn't want him to bear the burden of lying on my behalf. No doubt Mami would go straight to him once she realized I was missing. With everything else going on with Mikey, the last thing he needs is to take the fall for me. Keeping him in the dark is for the best.

"I'm going out with friends," I finally settle on.

"What friends?" he asks with a raised brow.

Rude, but fair.

"We're allowed to have friends," I say, as if that justifies me doing something I know is wrong—that I know'll hurt Mami. But I can't help feeling compelled to say it anyway. To remind Mikey of what Papi told me—that we deserve good things too.

"Okay," Mikey says, still sounding unconvinced. "Who is this friend?"

"Kai Thompson." I turn back around to try and go to jump off the ledge before he can question me more. But he manages to catch me by the arm before I can jump.

"Kai Thompson? Seriously? And since when do you need a duffle bag to 'hang out'?"

His words aren't harsh, and his grip is only as tight as it needs to be. A lump forms in my throat. Something about him reminds me of Papi. Solid, but soft. Mikey was always the most like Papi personality wise. Unlike me and Joel, he never had any trouble making friends and keeping them—lighting up rooms with his laugh. At least before Mami taught us to think of the world as something we should fear. Before life forced him to be hard. While I was born with the innate ability to blend in, Mikey was born to stand out. He still does, even now. But what once would've brought him popularity just puts a target on his back now. I think that's why he ends up in so many fights—people just can't seem to leave him alone.

When I turn to look at him now, all my resolve breaks down.

"We're going to his parents' cabin for the weekend. They have a place up in the woods near the river—but it's not a party. Just a few friends hanging out." I put as much heart as I can into my words, hoping he can see in my eyes just how desperately I need this. A break from our lives, even if it's just for a couple of days.

The guilt in my heart takes a new shape as I lock eyes with my baby brother. I can tell by the quirk of his lips and the furrow in his brow that he's going through the same complicated mix of emotions as I am. I've never been as close to him as I was to Joel, maybe because he felt so much younger than we were when we were so obsessed with the idea of getting older. Becoming adults with our own lives. And I realize now how this must look—me with one foot out the window. Running away from our house—from *him*. Leaving him alone with Mami in our dark, lonely house.

Part of me wonders if I should invite him. Show him that it's safe to go outside and live our lives like the teens we're meant to be. But something selfish holds me back, something scared, too. It's dangerous enough for me to go out on my own—who knows what would happen if two Sotos went missing.

Mikey eyes me skeptically as he lets go of me to cross his arms. "Who else is going?"

"Just his sister and some of her friends."

I know better than to mention Carla, but Mikey's able to put together the pieces on his own. He's been at Millcreek High for only two months, but everyone knows Kiki and Carla are a package deal.

"Carla?" he asks, already shaking his head before I can reply.

"May—"

"You can't go."

"Excuse me?" A laugh almost bubbles out of me. Usually I'm the one attempting some kind of authority. Keeping him in line whenever he gets into fights at school, warning him about what will happen if he keeps getting into trouble, but I've never felt less like the big sister than I do now. "Why not?"

"Because they're assholes!" Mikey says, loudly enough to set us both on edge. We keep our eyes glued to the door, me swinging my legs back into the room so I can jump down and shove my bag out of sight if I need to. But we're lucky—Mami didn't hear us. Yet.

"Those people *hate* us, Dina," Mikey whispers once we're sure the coast is clear.

I resist the urge to sigh. "Kai is different. He's sweet, and—"

"You barely know him," he snaps.

"You don't know that," I hiss, our faces nearly touching. Mikey's expression is hard, but his eyes betray him. He's scared—for me. In that moment, it takes everything in me not to break. To do exactly what Mami would want and crawl back home before I even leave.

Mikey sighs and collapses onto my bed with a soft "oof." "How do you know they don't have something planned? A prank or . . . something?" he asks, voice barely a whisper, the "or something" hanging heavy between us.

My gaze falls to the floor, focusing on a scuff on my shoe

instead of him. "I don't," I confess. "But I know Kai. I trust him. And that's enough for me."

He sits back up, reaching out to hold my wrist this time, but I pull away before he can grab me. "You shouldn't go," he insists as I swing my legs around the sill again.

"You sound like Mami," I reply before pushing myself to the edge of the sill again. If I don't leave now, I might miss Kai.

"Then let me come with you," Mikey presses, stepping up to the sill, ready to grab me if I leap.

"No," I hiss back. The thought of bringing him sours even more. Mikey coming to play bodyguard is just asking for something to go wrong.

"Then at least tell me where you're going."

"I . . ." I trail off, running low on energy to protest. Giving him the address means that either he or Mami could come after me and drag me back home. But I know how stubborn my baby brother can be—it's another reason why he keeps getting in fights even though I've told him over and over again that those assholes who pick on him aren't worth it.

"It's on North Albee Way. Near the lake," I tell him, keeping my answer vague. It's enough to satisfy him, though, and he gives me a tight nod that I take as my cue to leave.

The fall to the grass is quick, but the weight of my bag drags me down more than I thought. I hit the ground with a grunt—my knees buckling under the pressure. I'm narrowly able to catch my balance, bracing myself against the wall until I'm steady again. I stay frozen, pressed up against the red brick, waiting for Mami to scream or come banging out the front door to drag me back inside. Outside, there are birds chirping and the cicadas' night song. But no screams. No shouts to tell me to go back to my room.

When we're sure we're safe, Mikey sticks his head out the window, voice low and eyes softer. "Be careful, okay?" he whispers, lower lip quivering slightly. It's almost enough to make me crawl back inside just to hug him and promise no one's going to get hurt. *Almost.*

I swallow down the lump in my throat and my gut instinct. "I will."

Slowly, I make my way out of the darkness of our house. Mikey's focus is red-hot against my back as I cross the yard. The sky is a dusky orange that's perfect for trick-or-treating. Kids travel in clusters along the opposite block, huddled together as they sneak glances at our house. No one dares get too close. Some haunted houses aren't worth the price of admission.

I pull the hood of my sweater over my head and slide through the shadows until I reach the iron fence lining the edge of our property. I toss my bag over it before following along, making sure none of the kids on the opposite street notice me. Luckily, they are all too distracted with knocking on doors and trading candy. I glance behind me and watch as Mikey closes the window to my bedroom and disappears from view.

It's easy to get swept up in the Halloween buzz. Kids go barreling down the street in superhero costumes and princess gowns. Ghosts and devils haunt the streets, but a girl in a hoodie and torn jeans looking for a piece of normalcy is still the most threatening thing on the prowl tonight. Following the stream of people clamoring to the next street—wanting to get away from "that murderer's house" as quickly as they can—I look over my shoulder one last time before home disappears from view.

I'll be back soon, I say to myself. Like Papi said, I'm allowed good things. Even if the guilt threatens to eat me from the inside out, I deserve a few nights off from my life. A weekend where I'm not the daughter of a killer but a girl just like the hundreds of others in my class. Come Monday I'll be the real me again, but for now, it's enough to pretend.

6

The crowd parts around Kai like the sea. He's leaning up against his car, still wearing his Miles Morales costume from the dance. Sweat dots his brow despite the cool evening chill, and his smile is so radiant you'd think he'd just won the lottery. Fellow superheroes stop to ogle the detail in his costume—the latex so perfectly molded to his shape it's like it was created with him in mind.

"'Sup, Peter." Kai greets the little boy also dressed as Spider-Man with a fist bump, adding a salute for Captain America. The kids giggle to themselves before pulling Kai in for a selfie. He throws up a peace sign and sticks out his tongue playfully, the perfect image of a hometown hero.

While looking over the photo, Kai catches sight of me behind a coven of witches. Even with my hood pulled down over my face, he straightens up and waves me toward him. A new twinkle sparks in his eyes, but I don't let myself believe it's because of me.

"Look who showed up after all," he says once I reach him.

My starry-eyed grin falters. "Sorry, was I—"

"No, no, bad joke," Kai apologizes before I can finish. There's a rosy tint to his cheeks when he ducks his head sheepishly. "I'm glad you're here," he says so quietly I'm not sure if

I really heard it or just heard what I wanted to. But the smile he shoots me as he blinks up from beneath his thick, full lashes makes my heart pound so fast it doesn't matter if he did or didn't.

"You look . . ." I trail off, mouth dry as I struggle to find an adjective that isn't cringe, creepy, or worse: both. "Amazing," I finally settle on, and it's not an exaggeration either. The attention to detail in the costume is precise and intricate. The latex is stretched so tight across his toned body it makes my cheeks warm. It's clear from the fabric alone that this isn't some last-minute Party City costume. This is something that was made with time, love, and care.

Kai beams as he lifts up his left arm and flexes his biceps. He's far from the thick-as-a-brick muscles you expect from comic book heroes, but the bulge in his upper arm is still impressive enough to make me gulp.

"Made it myself," he says with a wink. "Took all of my summer job money and a few fights with Grandma's sewing machine, but I think it was worth it." He gestures to the spider emblem on his chest before looking up at me and quirking a brow, as if looking for approval.

"Definitely worth it," I say around a laugh, body as light as air within just a few seconds of seeing him again.

The sweetness of the moment is soured when I spot a group of kids in matching Minecraft costumes headed our way, heads bowed together as they whisper to one another—their eyes focused on me. In the rush of seeing Kai in his costume, I hadn't noticed that my hood had fallen away from my face. I quickly yank the hood back up, plastering on a too-tight smile for Kai and nodding my head toward his car.

"Ready to go?" I ask, hoping I don't sound as desperate as I am. I can feel the heat of the kids' eyes on me against my back. They won't do anything. They never do. But just because they aren't lunging at us doesn't mean they can't still hurt me.

There's no way Kai doesn't know about me, my family. Yet I'm still holding my breath for the moment he decides I'm not worth the effort. That one day he'll hear the whispers and see the way people glare at me and decide that he thinks I'm a monster, too. But for now, he just nods and says, "Here, let me take your bag."

After tossing my bag into the trunk, Kai heads to the driver's seat, and I'm prepared to slide in beside him up front, but a small white box is sitting on the seat. Kai picks it up before I can accidentally squash it, the flush returning to his cheeks once I've sat down and closed the door behind me.

"I know it's been almost two weeks, but I had to get you something," he explains before handing the box to me with a sheepish smile.

With my heart hammering in my chest, I delicately pull open the lid on the box, unsure what I'll find—bracing myself for a prank but hoping for the best. Nestled between layers of wax paper is a purple-and-orange-frosted cookie shaped like a bat. Above it, a marshmallow speech bubble with "boo!" written in chocolate frosting.

"Happy belated birthday," Kai says as I stare down at the cookie in open-mouthed shock.

I only snap out of my daze when he nudges his arm against mine, the simple touch making my skin ignite so suddenly I nearly jump out of my seat.

"You're not allergic to nuts or gluten or anything, are you?" he asks with wide-eyed concern. "I definitely should've asked you that first."

I shake my head softly, answering him by taking a bite out of the bat's left wing. It's delicious. Perfect. And as I break off a piece of the bat's other wing to share with Kai, watching him accept the offering with a smile that never fails to light up my day, I know that I didn't make a mistake coming out tonight. This weekend, and all its risk, will be worth it.

7

I'm used to silence. At home. At school. At the table I sit at by myself during lunch. But silence with Kai is different. Softer. Comfortable. At first I'm worried he'll be able to hear how hard my heart is pounding and how deeply I inhale every time he so much as switches on the turn signal, but once he hooks up his phone to the car's Bluetooth and queues up a playlist he says he listens to on his runs, I relax into my seat.

Ten minutes into the playlist I realize how painfully out of touch I am. My Spotify is a relic from our old life. Songs Papi would blast while he cleaned the bathroom on weekends, or that he used to motivate his teams while they ran laps. Old-school salsa and eighties ballads. Songs I stole off Joel's playlist that I would play through my headphones, head against the window, pretending I was the star of a moody teen drama.

Joel always had the best taste in music. The best taste in general. Even living in a house with so many rules, so closed off from everything, Joel managed to find other ways to experience the world. He was an artist, like Kai, but he preferred paints over pencils. And instead of heroes fighting crimes, he painted landscapes and detailed portraits—the places he dreamed of going one day, the people he thought he might meet. He also loved show tunes even though we knew our family didn't have the money to see a show on Broadway. But he loved how much emotion they could pack into a single song, how loudly they expressed themselves. He made the most of what our small, cramped world had to offer.

Thankfully, Kai's playlist is a very different vibe from Joel's, keeping me from getting lost in bittersweet memories. It's more high-energy, perfect for exercising, but I like the way the songs make me feel even just sitting down in a car. They're infectiously upbeat, like Kai himself.

We drive all the way to the edge of Millcreek. Past the road we usually turn off when we go to visit Papi, and toward the woods Mami always warned me to stay away from—like I could've gotten this far on my own. Still, her warning echoes in my ears as I swallow hard and sit up straighter.

Kai must notice my sudden nerves, lowering the music as he turns onto a narrow dirt road. "The others bailed on the dance so they're probably already up at the house by now," he explains. "You've met my sister, right?"

I shrug tightly. The closest Kiki and I have come to interacting was me stepping out of her way when she waltzed to the front of the cafeteria line earlier this year. "Sort of," I reply diplomatically. "Not officially."

"She's great," Kai says quickly, shooting me a smile before turning his attention back to the road. The car rattles as it drives over bumps and loose twigs, not helping the nausea building in my stomach at the thought of having to face Kiki and her friends. "And I'm sure she'll love you." I shoot Kai a skeptical look. "Seriously!" he insists. "I know she puts on this whole bad bitch act at school, but trust me, she's a huge softie." He slows down the car enough for him to lean across the dash and whisper, "Still sleeps with a night light and plushie."

I hold back a snort. The image of Kiki Thompson, star cheerleader and queen bee, sleeping with a stuffed animal and a butterfly-shaped nightlight is as absurd as me taking her place on the top of the cheerleading pyramid.

"But don't tell anyone that," Kai warns. "If she finds out I told, she'll murder me. And maybe you, too, so keep it quiet." He winks before holding his pinkie toward me. "Swear?"

I don't bother holding back my amusement as I slide my pinkie through his, ignoring the sparks that jolt through me when our fingers link. "You're too fun to get killed off," I reply with a smirk.

Kai beams, looking away from the road just long enough to meet my eyes and make my heart beat in triple time. He opens his mouth, but whatever he plans to say next is cut off by my phone buzzing in my lap. We both jump slightly in surprise, our hands whipping back to our respective spaces as I glance down at my phone.

Mikey.

Shit. Did Mami figure out I was gone already? Did he crack and tell her what I'd done—where I'd gone? I whip around to scan the back window of the car for any sign of Mami's SUV.

"Everything okay?" Kai asks as we turn off the main path onto a new, narrowly curved dirt road.

We're suddenly shrouded in darkness—thick clusters of trees blocking the last dregs of sunlight. The incoming call cuts off abruptly as I lose service. The car lurches over a large hole in the dirt road, which Kai quickly mumbles an apology for. If I didn't trust him, this would be the moment I'd realize something was wrong. Where I'd run away. But I don't.

"Sorry, just my brother," I finally reply to his earlier question, turning my phone over to avoid facing the One New

Voicemail notification. If he's anything like me, he sat stewing in his anxiety until he was convinced he made a mistake letting me leave and now wants to try to convince me to come back one more time.

Kai glances at me for a moment before turning his attention back to the view. "He's a freshman, right?"

I nod, surprised that he even knew Mikey existed. With how much we ignore each other at school, it wouldn't be surprising if people didn't know we were related at all.

"You two look alike," Kai says, a slight smile tugging at his lips. "Like your mom."

The shock of his words makes me gulp so hard I almost choke on my spit. How does he know Mami? Other than her shifts at the Costco forty-five minutes away, she's hardly ever outside.

More than that, though, I wonder what similarities he sees in us. So many people over the years have said that we are Papi's spitting image—enough for them to think we are as wicked as they believe he is. Besides our size, I've never thought Mami and I had much in common. Looks or personality wise. Then again, Mami has always been tough—the world gave her no choice. Something that's twisted over the years into stubbornness, a refusal to admit that she might be wrong. Couldn't the same be said about me, at least tonight? I don't have any reason to think I'm wrong about sneaking out tonight, but I can't say I wasn't stubborn about it, especially with Mikey.

Still, the thought of even that small, seemingly insignificant similarity is unsettling. The idea that I could become the wrong kind of stubborn someday. Or worse: I already am.

"Th-thanks," I murmur quickly before the silence can sit

for too long. Thankfully, Kai doesn't notice the unevenness of my voice as he focuses on the last stretch of road.

I shift to the edge of my seat as the cabin comes into view, my breath hitching as I take in the sheer size of it. Even from a distance it towers over the horizon. A large front porch with swings and wicker tables. Kayaks and paddle boards are abandoned beside the steps up to the porch. Twinkling lights are strung along the trees to light the way to the river. Music thumps from inside the cabin. As we get closer we can make out voices, see a small group gathered on the large, sprawling deck.

Kiki holds court from the center of the deck, vape in one hand and a red Solo cup in the other. Her loyal subjects, Carla Gutierrez and a boy I vaguely recognize as one of the jocks they both hang around, are filling their own cups with a mix of juices and liquors spread out across the glass table beside them. So much for this not being a rager.

Kai parks the car, and my eyes land on a rusty axe leaning up against a tree stump at the edge of the driveway, making my stomach drop. The handle is so worn it probably hasn't been used in ages, and it would probably fall apart if anyone tried. It's innocent. Just an old, forgotten piece of hardware here only to enhance the rustic vibe of the property. But it still makes my blood run cold. Memories of that night—blood on a blade—threaten to make me sick before I've even gotten out of the car. I feel a sudden urge to grab it—to take it and bury it somewhere in a shallow hole in the woods. Just to be safe.

"You good?" Kai asks, halfway out of the driver's seat.

I nod quickly, shaking my head and all those memories away, and give him my best, most confident smile. Once he closes the door behind him, I pull my phone back out and turn it off entirely—choosing to ignore the New Voicemail notification on the screen.

I'm gone. I'm safe. I'm fine, I repeat to myself like a mantra as I grab my bag from the backseat and shove my phone down as far as I can. Mikey can call me all he wants, but there's no going back now.

Kai opens the door for me, and I give him another polite smile as he guides me to the house, keeping my eyes carefully averted from the axe.

"Hey!" Kai calls out to the others, racing down the path to the deck and easily leaping up and over the railing like it's not a solid three-foot jump. "You guys remember Dina, right?"

The entire mood shifts the minute Kai says my name. Kiki and Carla stiffen, cutting off mid-conversation like my presence is a record scratch. The unfamiliar boy glances between Kai and his twin sister like he's watching a Ping-Pong match. I stay frozen to the ground, crossing my arms across my chest like they can guard my heart.

"Hey," I call out weakly, unsure what to do. There's no way I can make that jump like Kai—at least not without getting myself hurt—and I'm not sure the others want me any closer. I figured no one would be thrilled to see me, but I thought maybe they'd at least pretend for Kai's sake. That maybe the smaller setting, free from judging eyes, might make them kinder. But that was clearly wishful thinking, especially about Kiki Thompson and Carla Gutierrez.

I fight the urge to run back to the car and beg Kai to take me home as Carla gives me a searing once-over. I remind myself that I was invited here—Kai *wants* me here. I have just as much reason to be at this cabin as Carla and whoever the boy with the leering smile is.

“We’re gonna get more drinks,” Kiki announces, completely ignoring Kai’s question as she tugs Carla back into the cabin by the elbow, slamming the sliding door shut behind them.

Kai lets out a quick groan of frustration, softening when he glances over at me. “One sec,” he says before bolting into the cabin after his sister, leaving me alone with a stranger.

The boy gives me a ’sup nod in greeting before hoisting himself off his deep lawn chair. He has the typical high school jock look. Long, wavy brown hair with matching brown eyes. Strong arms and an even stronger jaw. His Brewers jersey rides up as he stretches, revealing a strip of his surprisingly well-defined abs. A move I’m sure has earned him many admirers at school.

“Don’t worry,” he says as he drops his arms back down and leans against the deck railing. “I don’t think your dad did it.”

With a smirk, he follows the others back into the cabin, leaving me with nothing but the trees, the distant hum of bugs, and the sound of my racing heart.

EXHIBIT E: TRANSCRIPT OF VOICEMAIL RECEIVED BY DINA SOTO FROM HER BROTHER, MICHAEL SOTO, AT 7:52 p.m. ON OCTOBER 31

MICHAEL SOTO: Dina. Mom came out to the kitchen. She doesn't know you're gone or anything, but she just told me about something that happened at work a-and . . . Shit, I think something might be going on. Call me back. Seriously. Don't fucking ignore me. I think they're planning something. The people you're with . . . You're not safe there.

8

The front door of the cabin is unlocked, but I hesitate on the doorstep for almost five minutes. Past the screen door I can hear the rumblings of Kai's and Kiki's voices. They chase each other throughout the cabin, their voices fading in and out before finally disappearing altogether. With a deep breath, I tighten my hold on my bag and open the door.

If I thought the cabin seemed impressive from the outside, it's nothing compared to the interior. Right off the front door, a large white sectional takes up most of the living room, with enough space to seat at least a dozen people around the mounted flatscreen—a TV so large it seems impossible for the wall to be able to hold all its weight. Behind the living room area is a startlingly white kitchen, complete with stainless-steel appliances so polished I can see my reflection gawking back at me as I walk past.

To the left of the kitchen, the sliding door to the deck is propped open. Art of various styles adorns each wall. Painted landscapes of beaches and coastal towns dotted with brightly colored buildings—places I've only ever seen in postcards. Some impressionist pieces of . . . well, I can't really tell what. Beside the door, a large glass bowl holds three sets of keys—one for each of the cars parked in the driveway.

I'd known the Thompsons were wealthy from the fact that Kiki and Kai each had their own cars, but it doesn't take much to seem wealthy in a town like Millcreek. We were able to make do with just Papi's coaching salary and the occasional jobs Mami took cleaning homes, and people around here are in a similar boat. But like most things when it comes to Kai, this feels like something pulled straight out of a movie. I pinch myself and close my eyes, prepared to wake up back home to Mami pounding on my door, telling me it's time to get ready for school. When I open them, I'm still here, watching Kai come down the stairs tucked away behind the living room.

"Sorry about her," Kai apologizes as soon as he sees me, running a hand along the smooth, shaved side of his head. "She's just in a weird mood today."

I highly doubt that, but I also know Kai is just trying to be nice and spare my feelings, so I don't argue as I follow him into the kitchen area.

There's an array of snacks spread out across the counter. Bags of chips and cookies, along with several liters of soda and bottles of what I recognize as the cheap tequila Papi would buy from the local gas station on rough days. I swallow hard at the sight of it. I still remember the stench of it on his clothes that night. The one that changed everything.

"They're going to come for me," he'd told Mami, who had started sobbing the minute he came through the door reeking of alcohol. We'd all known from the slump in his shoulders and the bags under his eyes what was going to happen. It was obvious from how the cops stopped by our house for questioning that he was their prime suspect. That it was only a matter of time until they gathered enough evidence to arrest him. As much as we argued and begged him to please, please,

please do something, he was gone by morning. All over the news by noon.

Kai must notice my unease. He follows my eyeline until he spots the alcohol on the counter, letting out a quiet groan before stomping toward the bottles. "I told them not to pull this shit," he mutters more to himself than to me as he scoops up as many of the bottles as he can and shoves them into the empty freezer. "The only reason Mom let us stay up here alone is because we promised we wouldn't be drinking."

Looks like I'm not the only one breaking my mother's rules tonight.

"Want anything to drink? Or eat?" he asks once the alcohol is safely out of view.

"M'fine," I mumble, giving him a weak smile. Even if the sight of the tequila hadn't made my stomach churn, it's still uneasy from the bumpiness of the last stretch of road to get here.

Kai nods, leaning against the fridge door as he scans the room. "Well, you can go get unpacked if you want?" he offers, gesturing to the staircase.

I nod eagerly. A few minutes of privacy is all I need to reset and shake off all thoughts of Mikey and Papi and Mami waiting for me back home. Once I've cleared my head, Kai and I can go back to the easy comfort that's always drawn me to him. If I'm lucky, Kiki might notice that—how easily we're able to relax into one another—and decide I might be worthy of staying after all.

Kai leads the way up the stairs, pointing to several of the framed photos along the way.

"This was from our parents' vow renewal last year," he says as he gestures to a photo of him, Kiki, and two people who must be their parents smiling together on the beach. They're carefully posed in front of an arch made of multicolored orchids, a pink and purple sunset stretched out across the calm, crystal-blue water behind them. It's the kind of photo you see inside empty picture frames—a promise that you too can have a life as fabulous as theirs.

"Our first summer here." The next photo is of the family posed on the front steps of the cabin. The string lights are missing, and there's no deck extending from the house. There's dust on the windows and holes torn in the screen door behind them, but their smiles say everything. That they and this house are full of possibilities.

"And the dance recital Kiki made us all sit through that summer," Kai explains as he gestures to the last photo before the second-floor landing. A middle-school-aged Kiki is dressed in a *Little Mermaid*–inspired ensemble, complete with a floor-length purple sequin skirt and seashell clips woven into her copper locs. She's at the center of a makeshift stage in what must be the backyard, the photo capturing her pointing and shouting directly at Kai, who's dressed as a crab. "I missed my cue."

I'm unable to hold back my laughter at the thought of crab-Kai getting chewed out by his sister. Something eases between the two of us as we laugh together, Kai's shoulders slackening and his smile carefree as he gestures for me to follow him down the hall. He rattles off the room assignments so quickly I miss the boy's name from earlier. The two of them will take the bunk beds in Kai's room, while Kiki and Carla will take the master.

"And you're the lucky visitor who gets the guest room all to herself," he says with a smile as he opens the door to the last room at the end of the hall. It's the smallest of the three rooms, but with its queen-size bed, desk, and plush armchair in the corner, it's still bigger than my room back home.

I set my bag down on the edge of the bed and collapse face-first into the mattress. The comforter is so soft it feels like it melts beneath my touch as I run my palms along it like I'm making a snow angel. The mattress could swallow me whole if I let it, and I'm very tempted to do just that. Sink in and disappear. The scent of lavender clings to the sheets as I bury my face and let my eyes slip closed. I'm midway through a deep whiff when a chuckle makes my eyes fly open.

"They're pretty great," Kai says before I can be mortified by him catching me acting like I've never been in a nice house before. For the most part, I haven't. But that's just another thing that sets me apart from him—and there are already enough tallies in that column. I don't need to add any more.

He slides onto the bed like it's nothing. Like we aren't lying horizontally together. Like his hand isn't resting barely an inch from my thigh. Like his lips aren't impossibly close—a breath apart from mine. I can see the moment it clicks for him as he looks up at me. When he realizes just how close we are. In the silence I swear I can hear his heartbeat, thrumming just as loud as mine. I blink and suddenly he feels even closer. So close it feels foolish not to lean forward and close the distance. But the door is open, and his sister is probably down the hall, and, and, and . . .

There might be a thousand reasons I shouldn't kiss him but my heart only wants to listen to the ones that say I should. I've already crossed one line to be here. And who knows if I'll ever be allowed to see him again come Sunday night? Maybe Mami will lock me away in my room and never let me leave again, even for school. If I'm going to kiss my freedom goodbye, I might as well have fun.

I sit up slightly, bracing myself with the hand resting between us, and lean forward when a familiar voice cuts through the silence.

"We're gonna watch a movie," Kiki announces, not looking at all fazed by catching her twin brother in a compromising position.

Kai and I fly to opposite ends of the bed—him moving so quickly he goes toppling over the edge and onto the ground. Kiki's smirk doesn't so much as crack as Kai hits the carpeted floor with a quiet *oof.* Carla suddenly appears over Kiki's shoulder, wearing a smile just as fiendish as her best friend's.

"You guys coming?" she asks with an arched brow as she looks at Kai before settling on me.

"Oh, uh, yeah, for sure," Kai says, sounding as flustered as I feel.

We both leap up, following closely behind Kiki as we head back down to the living room. The flutter in my heart doesn't stop, though.

Foolish as it might be, my hope for this weekend has been renewed. There's definitely something going on between Kai and me, and even if Kiki's initial reaction to me being here wasn't all that happy, maybe this movie invite is a step in the right direction. I doubt I'll be leaving here BFFs with her and Carla or anything, but I can't help but feel like this is a chance to show Kai that I can be as much a part of his world as any other girl, even with my past. That this weekend could change everything.

EXHIBIT F: TEXT MESSAGES BETWEEN KIKI THOMPSON AND CARLA GUTIERREZ ON OCTOBER 31

CARLA: omw to the cabin
KIKI: bitch why are you always an hour late
CARLA: chill we went to buy shit
CARLA: I got the stuff
KIKI: what stuff???
CARLA: 🐷
KIKI: omg WHAT where did you find it?!!!
CARLA: Costco
KIKI: wtf why do they have that at Costco
CARLA: costco has everything bitch!!!
KIKI: ok ok just store it in the shed when you get here
CARLA: 😘😘😘

9

"I'm Carla, by the way," Carla says as we reenter the living room, as if I wouldn't already know who she was.

What catches me off guard is the ease in her tone. Light and airy in a way that doesn't seem possible for a girl who regularly makes people cry if they so much as look at her the wrong way. And especially not toward me—someone she has history with.

We haven't interacted since Papi's trial, though we hardly ever interacted before that either. The cameras loved her almost as much as she loved them—the young, beautiful grieving girlfriend. She'd played her part perfectly, dabbing her tears with a monogrammed handkerchief every time a camera was shoved in her face. Sang the praises of her now-dead boyfriend, about how she was sure they were going to be forever—even though everyone knew they'd broken up nearly a month before the murder. With a story as juicy as my father's, though, the newscasters didn't bother to fact-check the teen drama side of the matter.

Still, I wouldn't blame her for hating me. It's hard seeing a reminder of someone you lost every day.

Carla slinks across the room to slide into the unfamiliar boy's lap. His arms instantly snake around her waist as he presses a sloppy kiss to her neck—the gesture strangely heated considering they're in front of an audience. Beside me, Kiki rolls her eyes while Kai shifts uncomfortably.

"And this is my boyfriend, Timothy," Carla explains on his behalf, playfully pulling down the brim of his ballcap when he continues trying to glom onto her like a dog in heat.

Finally, the pieces click into place. Timothy Gibson, captain of the football team and the subject of several summons to the principal's office over the PA loudspeaker. Sports have never interested me, even when Papi was at the helm of the Millcreek soccer team, so my knowledge of Timothy beyond his name and status is limited. From what I can tell, he's equal parts talented and troublesome. And, apparently, Carla's boyfriend.

They fit together well, even aside from their cheerleader and football player labels. Like Kiki, Carla Gutierrez is the type of beautiful that skyrockets you to the top of the social pyramid. With her thick, dark hair trailing down to her lower back and dewy light brown skin, she looks perfectly sun kissed in a town defined by its overcast skies. I can't remember the last time we had multiple days of sunshine in a row—even in summer—but you'd never guess it from the glow radiating off Carla. She doesn't seem bothered by the slight October chill either, dressed in a Guns N' Roses crop top and cutoff shorts with a flannel tied around her waist. Together, she and Timothy look like the kind of couple girls like me long to be in. The type whose photos you see splashed across manifestation boards because they have the perfect carefree teenage aesthetic.

Over Carla's shoulder, Timothy's eyes find mine, and he shoots me a lazy smile that makes my cheeks flush.

"Nice to meet you," I say with a tight-lipped smile, unsure

what to do. Offering a hand to shake feels too formal and a wave feels too childish, so instead I shove my hands into the pockets of my sweater. As Carla swings her legs off Timothy's lap and crosses the room to the flatscreen, I realize I forgot to actually introduce myself. *They all know who you are, what you are*, a voice that sounds unsettlingly like Mami's whispers in my ear.

Before I can dwell on that thought, Carla flips the TV on and starts scrolling through the various streaming apps on the home screen.

"How scary are we thinking?" Carla asks as she opens up Netflix and navigates straight to the horror section. "Actually scary, or so-cheesy-it's-hilarious scary?" She hovers between two options—one, a low-budget slasher about a killer ventriloquist dummy, and the other an experimental folk horror about a demon haunting an Austrian village.

"Actually scary," Timothy says at the exact same moment Kiki says "cheesy."

Kai and I stay quiet while Kiki and Timothy stare each other down. Kiki's brow furrows, her glare so piercing I'd probably melt on the spot if it was directed at me. Timothy, though, just holds his hands up in surrender.

"Have it your way, wimp," he says before pulling a joint and a lighter out of his pocket.

"Outside," Kiki snaps before Timothy can flick the flame to life, snatching the joint out of the corner of his mouth. "We're not getting grounded for a month because you decided to stink up the place."

Kai nods in agreement as Timothy rolls his eyes before begrudgingly picking himself up off the couch. "Fine," he mutters, waving his hand lazily as he trudges toward the sliding door leading to the back deck. He pauses, taking in Kai's costume properly for the first time.

"Dude, weren't you Spider-Man for Carla's birthday party?"

Kai bristles at the question. I don't have social media of my own—Mami didn't allow it, and I count it a blessing after the Papi incident—but that hasn't stopped me from checking in on my classmates. I can vaguely remember shots of Kai in the background of the various photos Carla posted over the summer from her annual birthday costume party.

"When there's another Black and Puerto Rican superhero then I'll be them instead," he replies defiantly, puffing his chest out slightly with pride.

Timothy brushes Kai off with a wave of his hand and murmurs a lazy "all good" before sauntering toward the sliding doors to the deck.

"Don't wait for me. I've already seen this one anyway." Timothy turns around, arms outstretched and the joint hanging from the corner of his mouth again as he announces, "Spoiler: it's all a dream."

"Go outside, asshole," Kiki calls over her shoulder while Carla tosses a throw pillow at Timothy's head in annoyance.

Kai shrugs as he flops onto the couch and picks up the remote from where Carla tossed it aside. "Don't worry, I know another one that'll work." He navigates slightly down the page until he's settled on something called *Filomena's Revenge*. The screen fills with a silent trailer for the movie, yet another low-budget slasher but this time with an army of knock-off Muppets.

"Twice the puppets, twice the gore, and three times the cheese," Kai explains, hitting play once Kiki gives him a thumbs-up in approval, but pauses it as soon as the movie loads.

Kiki busies herself with pouring a new drink while Kai

excuses himself to his room to change into something more casual.

"Make me one," Carla calls out to Kiki as she crosses toward the deck. "I'll be right back." She slips out the sliding door and through the mesh and glass I can see her lean up against the deck railing, swipe the blunt out of Timothy's mouth, and take a long drag.

Kiki rolls her eyes but obliges Carla's request and pours enough tequila into a fresh cup to churn my stomach again.

"You want one?" Kiki asks, her gaze so vacant as she looks in my general direction that I wouldn't be sure she was talking to me if I wasn't the only person left in the room.

Kai returns before I can answer, having switched into a pair of sweats and a flannel in record time. Kiki swivels around to face him, making him the same offer with a lot more enthusiasm than she had for me.

"I'm good," he says quickly before flopping onto the couch beside me, leaning in to lightly nudge his shoulder against mine. "It's okay if you want some," he whispers. "Or if you don't. Either's cool."

Rosiness tints his cheeks as he shrugs and leans back against the couch, while Kiki waits impatiently for an answer. The fact that I can make someone like him blush feels impossible. So impossible that I peek over my shoulder at him to make sure I didn't imagine it. But there he is: hiding his flushed cheeks against the couch as he aimlessly plays with a loose thread on the throw pillow.

"No, thanks," I tell Kiki. Even if the thought of alcohol didn't make me feel uneasy, the last thing I need is the type of buzz that'll make me sloppy. It'll be easy enough for me to embarrass myself without the influence of alcohol.

Kiki shrugs before pouring the last of the bottle into her own cup, topping it with a mix of various sodas, and settling onto the opposite end of the couch from us.

Along the way she flicks off the last of the overhead lights, bathing the room in darkness before unpausing the movie. If it weren't for the glow from the TV, the room would be pitch-black—completely dark except for the distant glow of the string lights in the reflection of the sliding-glass door. The thought of trying to find my way around in the middle of the night—looking for the bathroom or a glass of water from the kitchen in the dark—makes me swallow hard.

The movie starts in silence, opening on a serene shot of a quaint house on a secluded patch of forest—not unlike this one. Even straining my ears there's no sound to make out. No distant grasshoppers or chirping birds. No crunch of gravel and dirt as cars drive past. Not even murmured snippets of Timothy and Carla's conversation on the deck. All I can hear is my own unsteady breathing as I sink farther into the couch and wring my fingers together. I've watched my fair share of horror movies, but they've never unsettled me this much before. Then again, I've never been in a cabin in the middle of the woods with a bunch of strangers before, either.

Maybe it's not the movie that has me so on edge.

Part of me hopes Kai will move closer. That he'll notice my nervousness and wrap an arm around me or let me cower on his shoulder. We both jump slightly as the calm opening scene is interrupted by a jump scare of a killer puppet lunging at a woman biking down a dirt path, but stay a careful, respectful distance apart.

"There's no way that actually scared you," Kiki taunts with a raised brow.

"Jump scares are cheap but effective," Kai replies with a raised finger. "And I'm not too proud to admit they scare the shit out of me."

I nod in agreement as Kiki scoffs and turns back to the screen. We settle back into silence as we focus on the movie, my heartbeat evening out once the scene shifts to a stereotypical high school setting.

But it doesn't take long for the tension to creep back. Within minutes of introducing us to our lead, we find him alone in a darkened computer lab in search of his missing friend. The music quiets until we're left with nothing but subtle violin shrieks, growing louder and louder until suddenly—

Someone sits down beside me.

"Chill, it's just me," Timothy says around a laugh when I let out a scream, holding his hands up in surrender.

My heart doesn't calm even with his reassurance. He's slightly too close for comfort—the edge of his knee brushing against mine. Close enough that the scent of earth and dry leaves overwhelms me—a scent I recognize from gym class, wafting out from behind the bleachers. His eyes are half-lidded, and I can see the reddish tinge to the whites of them even in the dark. His voice is softer, lazier as he settles back against the couch cushions and spreads his arms wide. I shift a polite distance away from him, but unless I want to encroach on Kai's space, there's no way for me to get fully away from the expanse of Timothy's arms. I settle back carefully, hovering just above the couch cushions to avoid having his fingertips brush against my shoulder.

"Where's Carla?" Kiki asks as she peers back toward the deck.

Timothy shrugs, finally pulling his arm back to reach for a bag of Cheetos on the coffee table in front of us. I quickly lean back and claim my spot while I can. He pops the bag open and pours the Cheetos directly into his open mouth. "Had to call her mom or something. She'll be back in a second," he says around a bite so huge I wouldn't have thought it humanly possible.

Kiki wrinkles her nose while Kai shudders at the sight. Timothy munches happily on his Cheetos while the rest of us turn back to the movie. He finishes off most of the bag in just a few handfuls—orange dust staining his fingertips and the front of his shirt. He leans toward the edge of the couch, keeping the all-white suede fabric of the cushions safe from the dust. Just as he leans back to settle in, Kiki shoots him yet another glare.

"Don't even think about it," she mutters, pointing to a stack of napkins on the coffee table.

Timothy groans like a punished toddler but heeds Kiki's warning. After wiping off his fingertips he flops back onto the couch with a burp.

Any hopes I had that he'd settle somewhere farther away from me are crushed the second he leans back. I do my best to get out of his path, but he still lands so close that his knee knocks against mine on the way down. His palm winds up in the space between us, his pinkie finger close enough to brush the edge of my thigh.

My breath catches in my throat at the sudden closeness. Unlike earlier with Kai, the oppressive scent and heat of him isn't welcome in my space. I resist the impulse to push him away. Clearly he's not in his right mind. He probably didn't mean to sit so close to me—especially with his girlfriend coming back any second.

It's absurd that I even thought it—that he sat next to me intentionally. That he *wants* to be close to me. Boys like him don't creep up on girls like me. Don't let their pinkies slide over toward them when they feel safe under the shroud of the dark.

I glance at Kai out of the corner of my eye, but he doesn't seem to notice the closeness between me and Timothy. It's probably too dark for him to even see. Kiki is occupied with her phone, and Timothy focuses on the movie as much as someone as high as he is can. I consider excusing myself to the bathroom just to have a reason to leave when an earsplitting sound makes us all rocket up to attention. Suddenly, something pounds against the back wall—close to the sliding door, followed quickly by that same sound again.

The sound, I realize with a gulp, of someone screaming.

10

Kiki immediately jumps into action.

"Carla?!" she shouts, hurrying toward the deck while Kai pauses the movie and scrambles to flip on the overhead lights.

Everything is a blur as I stay frozen on the edge of the couch. I will myself to move—to at least turn around so my neck doesn't cramp from twisting to look at the sliding doors behind me.

Timothy is too stoned to fully comprehend what's going on, but he does his best to stumble off the couch and toward the deck. I breathe easier once he's no longer pressed up beside me, but it's impossible to relax with that frantic pounding on the walls. Even with the room flooded with light again we can't make out what's going on. Outside the sun has fully set, leaving the woods past the windows and doors as pitch-black as it had been inside moments earlier.

"Carla!" Kiki calls out again, struggling to pry open the sliding door. No matter how hard she tugs, the door doesn't budge. Her knuckles go white from the effort of gripping the handle with all her strength, her breath coming out in short, labored bursts as she tugs and tugs but doesn't get any movement. "This fucking thing is jammed again!"

Kai whips around and throws the front door open, making

a dash for the deck from outside of the cabin. Finally, I snap out of my daze. Lunging off the couch, I move for the door—but I hesitate in the wide-open entryway. Mami's voice rings in my ears again.

Never go chasing after trouble, she'd warned Mikey after he landed his first detention for picking fights with boys at school. Ignoring that he was provoked—that they'd called him all the same horrible things they'd called me, called Papi. He just hadn't learned how to walk away from them yet. And still hasn't. She'd leaned in across the dining table, eyes narrowed as she whispered so low we had to strain to hear her. *Unless you want to walk into a trap.*

Still, it feels cowardly, staying inside when someone is shouting for help. Part of me itches to go after Kai, to hold him back until we're sure where the screams are coming from, but the pounding and wailing cuts off before I have to make that call.

Laughter echoes around us.

"What the hell, Carla?" I can hear Kai shout from somewhere in the direction of the deck.

When I turn around, Kiki has given up on trying to pull open the sliding door. Light spills out across the deck as the string lights flicker back to life. A disgruntled Kai hoists himself over the deck railing followed by Carla, holding her stomach while doubled over with laughter.

"I'm sorry," Carla says in between laughs, tears streaming down her cheeks. "I had to."

"You didn't have to do anything," Kiki snaps, pulling the door open with ease, and then grabbing Carla by her arm hard enough for her laugh to cut off abruptly.

"Watch the hair," Carla whines, tugging her pin-straight

hair out from where it's trapped under Kiki's tightly closed fist. She brushes the hair over her shoulder casually before pinching Kiki's cheeks between her glossy, manicured fingers. "Your face was so worth it."

Kiki slaps Carla's hand away—the sound echoing through the room. I wince at the harshness of it, but Carla doesn't seem to mind. She slinks over to the kitchen, grabbing an abandoned drink off the counter and taking a long swig.

"Who cares about the movie," she says as if she hadn't been the one to suggest it. "We should be in the hot tub."

Everyone except Timothy eyes one another skeptically. Kai had told me to pack a bathing suit, but I'd hoped that with the late fall chill it would be too cold to actually get any use. Kiki doesn't seem convinced and neither does Kai, a theory that's confirmed when he turns to shoot me a questioning raised brow. Before I can shrug in reply, Carla scoffs and throws her hands up in the air.

"What?" Carla smirks as she gestures to the barely lit-up deck. Besides the string lights and the faint glow of the controls on the hot tub, it's almost impossible to see five feet past the cabin. "Are you wimps too scared to go outside in the dark?"

The taunt makes Kiki bristle and cross her arms. "You literally just scared the shit out of us."

"Oh, please! That was the most cliché trick in the book," Carla whines before slinging an arm around Kiki's shoulders. "C'mon, it's almost Halloween, and *you* were the one who wanted to skip out on the dance, so . . ." She runs a finger along Kiki's bare arm. Even from across the room I can see the way goose bumps blossom along the path of Carla's touch. "You owe me a good time."

Kiki stiffens when Carla's fingers curl around her shoulder, glaring down at the bracelet on her best friend's wrist—*Carla* written in cursive on a long gold plate, a delicate chain linked on either side—before wriggling out of her grip.

"Fine," Kiki mutters as she snatches the cup out of Carla's hand, downs it in one long gulp, then crushes it in her fist. She tosses it into the trash as she crosses the room, headed toward the staircase. "We'll meet on the deck in five," she commands, and that's all Carla and Timothy need to smirk and rush upstairs to change.

Across the room, Kai sighs as he steps in from the deck. He runs a hand through his hair, his brow wrinkled like he's aged a dozen years since we got here barely an hour ago. Our relaxing weekend getaway is already proving to be more chaotic than I anticipated, and we've only just arrived. I haven't been to many—well, any—parties. Or sleepovers either. Mami would send me to the moon before a stranger's house for an overnight stay. But from the slumber parties I'd seen on TV, our night is only just getting started.

"You brought a bathing suit, right?" Kai asks me after he's closed the sliding door behind him.

I nod, cheeks flushing at the thought of the two-piece I'd shoved to the bottom of my bag, hoping it wouldn't see the light of day.

This time, Kai senses my hesitance, taking a step toward me but remaining a careful distance away. "And you're still okay with this?" he asks in a measured whisper, looking over his shoulder to gesture to the Solo cups sitting on the counter and the vague scent of weed lingering in the air. "I know all of this isn't really your scene."

I nod again, surer this time. Feeling more at ease just from the knowledge that he's not pushing me any farther than I'm willing to go. "I'm sure," I say, biting my lip as I look up at his soft, sincere eyes.

"All right . . ." Kai backs away slowly, looking unconvinced until I give him a smile. The tension melts off him, his own smile bubbling up as he makes it to the staircase. "I'll meet you at your room and we can head down together?"

Together. Such a simple word—a simple concept—and yet my heart swells at the thought of it. Us. Together. It overwhelms me to the point that I'm frozen in place until Kai heads up the stairs and disappears from view, and I finally let out the breath that hitched when he walked away.

11

The person standing in front of the mirror doesn't look anything like me. The last time our family drove out to the sleepy lakeside town where half of Millcreek spends their summers was at least three years ago. Before my body had sprouted seemingly overnight. Back then, I was all flat planes and straight lines. Freckled skin and pigtail braids.

As I turn to examine myself from the side, I can't help but linger on the swell of my hips, and the way the skintight fabric clings to my body. It's easy to forget I have any sort of shape when all I wear are Mami's hand-me-downs. I never minded the baggy T-shirts and sweaters. Maybe if I let my clothes swallow me whole, nobody would notice me. But there's something thrilling about seeing myself—the me I'd forgotten existed—in my reflection. Practically a stranger. With a smile so wide I'd never think it was me if she didn't match my movements.

I pulled my hair out of its braid to fall loose and free along my shoulder, my curls trailing down to just above my belly button. My skin isn't dewy and flawlessly radiant like Carla's, but I'm not as pale as the fluorescent lighting at school and Sunny Hills makes me seem. Like with the dress I stole for my birthday, I run my fingertips along the neckline of the swimsuit and marvel at the person I could be. The body I have but never let myself show. I feel strong. I feel captivating. I feel *beautiful.*

And I feel like an imposter.

Even if the tags for this swimsuit weren't digging into my skin, I'd still feel like I was living a lie. This isn't me—who I'm allowed to be. The girl with the thick, luscious hair that you long to run your fingers through. The girl with curves like winding roads and a smile that stops traffic. I'm the girl who had to swipe this outfit from the mall last week because there wasn't anything left in my own dresser that would actually fit my post-puberty body.

It was easier this time—swiping the swimsuit off its hanger and shoving it into my bag. By the time I slipped out of the store no one had even noticed that I'd left the dressing room. Finally, my talent for keeping my head down and staying under the radar actually came in handy.

After looking myself over one last time, I dab on a light layer of lip gloss and grab one of the towels sitting on the top of the dresser. As promised, Kai is waiting for me outside my room when I open the door, leaning up against the wall, arms crossed against his bare chest, wearing a loose, unbuttoned linen shirt. I stall in the doorway, hand limp around the knob as I try to take all of him in without making it obvious just how hopeless I am.

His arms are lean, but firm. Not bulging with muscles like Timothy's or the other jocks from the football team but undeniably strong. A slim silver cross sits at the base of his collarbone, twinkling even in the dim overhead lighting. His smile when he sees me could light up the entire sky, and makes me feel lighter than air.

"You look great," he says as he kicks off the wall.

"You do too," I reply so quickly my cheeks flush.

Kai ducks his head sheepishly as he looks down at his own ensemble. "Wasn't sure whether to go with or without the shirt." He tugs on the collar of his baby blue linen shirt before gesturing down to his chest. "Since, y'know. Scars," he mumbles sheepishly.

I hadn't noticed the scars, laced along the left and right sides of his chest, until he pointed them out. They're healed enough that the surgery couldn't have been super recent, but haven't begun to fade just yet. There's a strangely beautiful symmetry to the way the scars are woven on top of one another, wound together like ribbons.

He runs a hand down the back of his neck and suddenly averts his gaze from mine. This is a new type of shyness from him, a raw vulnerability. I was already longing to run my fingers along the smooth plane of his chest, but I ache for it with a new hunger now. To show him he has nothing to hide—not from me or the rest of the world.

I can understand his hesitancy, though. When he and Kiki first transferred to Millcreek, they were the center of gossip for weeks. Rumors about who they were and why they'd transferred flew through the halls at the speed of light, morphing and evolving into everything from them being in the witness protection program to them being undercover FBI agents sent to investigate an illegal drug ring. But pieces of the truth slipped through the cracks.

When word spread that Kai was trans, I found myself on edge whenever I saw him in the halls. Not because that changed how I felt about him, but I'd seen the way my classmates responded to queerness. How cruel people could be about something as simple as who you are. I'd seen how dark things could become—how far our classmates were willing to go to hurt someone. The thought of them hurting Kai made me sick to my stomach. Watching the same people who tortured Joel wipe away the confidence and laughter and joy in this boy who managed to brighten my day with a single smile was not something I wanted to witness. But I knew I couldn't actually do anything. Having the girl with the murderer for a dad stand up for him would only put a bigger target on his back.

But no one lashed out at him. No one taunted him or called him names or cornered him after school. Within a few weeks he and Kiki had taken their places at the top of the social hierarchy. Two weeks later, Kai was homecoming king, something that would've seemed impossible just a year earlier. Things had shifted—either out of fear of what happened the last time students had targeted someone, or because Kai was the type of person that was impossible to dislike. Last time, they had an easy target. Someone who was quiet and shy and afraid of the world because that's what he was raised to believe. A blank slate for them to project all their hatred onto.

For better or for worse, my classmates had learned their lesson. They wouldn't make the same mistakes again.

Not after Joel.

I realize I've let the silence sit for too long when Kai reaches for the top button of his shirt. Shaking off the memory of my brother, I quickly take a step toward Kai.

"I think they're beautiful."

The compliment makes him bloom like a flower in spring. He lets go of the collar of his shirt and I don't even realize his fingers have slid through mine until his thumb grazes along my knuckles. Kai's lips part slightly, but whatever he's about to say is cut off.

"Damn, Soto," Timothy exclaims as he steps out of his

room across the hall. "That's what you've been hiding under all those hoodies?" He leans up against the wall beside us and shamelessly takes me in from head to toe.

I quickly pull my hand out of Kai's to cross my arms across my chest, suddenly feeling like I'm not wearing anything at all.

"Don't be an ass," Kai warns, quickly standing in front of me, shielding me while I drape my towel over my body.

Timothy scoffs and rolls his eyes as he brushes past Kai. "Just admiring the view."

Kai doesn't let him walk away that easily though, giving him a light shove on the arm. Not enough to make him stumble, but enough to make him pay attention. "Why don't you go *admire* your girlfriend?"

"Whoa, whoa." Timothy holds his hands up in surrender, brows pinched. Despite his peaceful gesture he shoves Kai back with twice as much force—knocking him back into me. "Watch yourself, bud."

"Watch *your*self," Kai snaps back, looking as though he's going to lunge.

I reach out to grab his arm before he can retaliate, not wanting things to escalate into a full-on fight—over *me*, no less. Though Kai doesn't seem like he's a fan of Timothy in general. Based on the way Timothy is glaring at him, the feeling might be mutual.

"Whatever," Timothy says, rolling his eyes before heading down the stairs.

As soon as he's out of view Kai lets out a harsh exhale. The tension in his body eases beneath my touch like a knot coming undone.

He shakes his head, pacing in a line before stopping in front of me. "Shit, I'm *so* sorry. I knew he was a dick but I didn't . . ."

He trails off, unsure how to finish that sentence as his gaze falls to the floor. When he looks back up, his eyes linger on where my fingers are gripping the towel so tightly my knuckles have gone as white as the towel itself. "Are you okay?"

I nod quickly, relaxing my hold now that we're alone. "M'fine."

Kai glances out a window behind us, overlooking the deck. Through the glass we watch as Timothy steps outside with his arms thrown high in the air, like a god greeting his mortal subjects. Neither Kiki nor Carla give him the time of day, even after he flops into the hot tub with enough force to send a wave splashing onto the deck. Kiki scolds him with a punch to his arm while he buries his face in Carla's neck and attempts to steal her drink with his free hand.

"We can skip the hot tub if you want," Kai offers with a sheepish smile. "Stay in and finish that movie."

While the thought of staying inside *does* sound more appealing than facing Timothy again, I can't imagine that'll buy me any favor with the group. I'm not really here to make friends, but Kiki is Kai's twin sister. She will always be in his life, a constant I could never come between. And avoiding her won't help convince her that I'm worthy of Kai's time and attention. If I want a future with Kai, that also means a future with Kiki.

"I'm okay." I give him my best smile before starting toward the staircase, the smile faltering the second I'm out of his line of sight.

Kai doesn't let me make it far. He reaches out for my arm and whirls me around, sliding his arm up to grip my shoulders as he steps in closer to me. "I promise I won't let him get near you, all right?"

His words make my insides glow as warm as the fairy lights strung up outside. I resist the urge to hold my pinkie up between us—to make him promise the way Papi always did when I was little. But that memory, like so many, is soured.

Promise me you'll come home, I whispered to him the night before the cops took him, the scent of tequila still on his breath as he whispered back that he would. Always would. It was a promise he couldn't keep, but he took my pinkie in his anyway.

I offer Kai a nod instead. "All right."

With my reassurance, Kai runs his fingertips gently down the slope of my arm until he reaches my hand, linking our fingers again. It would be so easy to lose myself in how perfectly we seem to slot together. When he tugs me gently toward the stairs, I follow as if I'm floating on a cloud, all thoughts of Timothy and his wandering eyes and Papi and his broken promises left behind.

12

Even with the string lights on, the deck is startlingly dark. If the others are put off by it, they don't let it show. Carla has connected her phone to a Bluetooth speaker on the glass table beside the grill, blasting a song I vaguely recognize and swaying to the beat as she pours herself a fresh drink. At the far edge of the hot tub, Timothy takes a long drag from his vape pen while Kiki is perched on the opposite side of the tub, focused on telling Carla how to make her drink properly.

"That's enough!" She waves her hand until Carla lifts up the can of pineapple juice. "I said a *splash* of pineapple."

"That shit's gonna give you cavities," Timothy says with a lazy grin, blowing his cherry-scented smoke in my and Kai's direction. He welcomes us to argue against him with a smirk that makes my skin crawl, but neither of us takes the bait.

"It wouldn't if Carla made it right," Kiki mutters bitterly under her breath.

Carla whips around and stomps her foot like a toddler. "I did exactly what you said, you're just—"

Kai breaks up the potential fight by standing between Kiki and Carla before their bickering can get any louder. He puts a gentle hand on his sister's shoulder and grabs the drink from Carla with his free hand.

"Can we say thank you to Carla for making you this drink so you didn't have to get your lazy ass out of the water?" he asks his sister with a raised brow.

Kiki sucks her teeth as she wriggles out from under his grip. "Don't talk to me like I'm a fucking five year old."

"Then stop acting like one," he snaps back.

"Ugh, you sound like mom." Kiki rolls her eyes and snatches the cup out of his hand. Despite her complaints, she downs half the drink in one gulp. She lets out a ragged breath and wipes pineapple juice from the corner of her mouth before turning to look at Carla. "Give him a shot," she instructs before turning to her brother with her usual apathetic gaze. "You're killing the vibe."

Kai seems annoyed, but he doesn't protest Kiki's dismissal or her command. Following orders, Carla delivers a generous shot of tequila to Kai. He wrinkles his nose after he takes a whiff of the drink, looking hesitant for a moment before gulping it down as quickly as his sister had seconds earlier. He winces the second the alcohol passes his lips, face scrunched up in disgust even after he's swallowed it down. I don't realize how roughly I'm biting down on my lip until a jolt of pain forces me to ease up.

"Just needed to take the edge off," he whispers to me after setting the cup on the table and returning to my side. His voice is ragged, like Kiki's had been moments earlier, and his cheeks are still flushed.

I'm not mad at him for drinking, though I can see how he thought I was. I just can't stomach it. That too-familiar smell—harsh and acidic and sharp as knife. As he shrugs out of his shirt and steps into the hot tub, I catch the scent of his cologne clinging to his skin. Somehow that smell—the scent of cologne mixed with the tequila—is worse.

Papi's cologne always lingered too.

"Are you getting in or just standing there?" Kiki asks, snapping me back to reality.

Kai scolds her by splashing in her direction. Kiki lets out a scream that could wake the dead as she tucks a loose loc hanging in front of her face behind her ear and out of harm's way. The rest of her hair is held back in a chic patterned hair clip, held more securely by a silk scarf that's almost the exact same shade of lilac as her bikini. It's identical to Carla's suit except for the color—Carla opting for fire engine red.

As I quickly shuffle into the hot tub before I can embarrass myself again, Carla follows my lead and steps into the tub too. I breathe a sigh of relief as she settles down beside Timothy, his arm draped across her shoulders. Once again, he buries his face in her neck, but she doesn't pay him any mind.

"Like what you see?" she asks with a smirk, and I don't even realize the question is aimed at me until I look away from the strap of her bikini to find her eyes locked on mine.

"Can you guys leave her alone for five seconds?" Kai interjects before I can reply, hovering in the water between me and Carla, protecting me like a shield or a guard dog.

If I thought the water was warm before it's nothing compared to the combined heat of Kai's closeness and Carla's teasing gaze. I'm so hot all over I feel like I could melt any second, my skin prickling with a combination of anticipation and mortification.

"It's fine," I assure Kai, straightening myself out before turning to give Carla my most sincere smile. "That's a nice color."

She meets my smile with a pleased look, her lips curling around the rim of her cup. "Thanks."

"Did you and Kiki buy them together?" I ask. Carla responds with a confused raised brow. I turn to Kiki, gesturing toward her own bikini before adding, "They're the same swimsuit, right?"

Carla and Kiki exchange a loaded, too-long look that sets me on edge the longer it lasts. Kai glances between the two of them while Timothy blinks at his girlfriend like he's seeing her from underwater, his eyes tinged red and pupils blown as wide as the full moon shrouded behind the clouds.

Finally, after what feels like hours Carla breaks the silence with, "We have the same taste" at the exact same moment Kiki says, "We should play a game."

The girls lock eyes again after the overlap, Kiki mouthing something so quick I can't make it out, but Carla gets the message loud and clear.

"Never Have I Ever?" she suggests without missing a beat, moving on as if nothing happened between the two of them.

The whiplash of the conversation leaves me reeling. While I've never played this game before I've seen it on TV enough times to know how it works—and that I'll be embarrassingly awful at it. Before I can even think of another game to suggest, Kiki leans out of the tub enough to reach the table and pour a fresh drink for everyone—a mix of Bacardi and Diet Coke. Before I can politely turn down the drink, she shoves a cup into my hand.

No one explains the rules once drinks are in hand. Kiki takes her rightful place at the center of our semicircle, holding up her claw-like fingers and looking around at each of us with a smirk before kicking the game off.

"Never have I ever . . . gotten detention," she says with a pleased smile to a round of groans.

"Bitch," Carla mutters before shoving her pinkie down. Beside her, Timothy tucks his thumb into his palm with a scoff.

"Not my fault you're a delinquent," Kiki preens, lifting up her drink in a toast as both Carla and Timothy take delicate sips of their own.

Once he's downed his punishment sip, Timothy leans back against the edge of the tub and tilts his head up. His eyes glaze as he takes in the night sky and his brows furrow, deep in thought the way only someone who's stoned can be.

"Never have I ever . . ." He pauses for so long Carla has to shove him to get him to even attempt to finish his statement. "I don't know. Stolen something." He shrugs and slumps back until half of his face is submerged beneath the water.

Carla turns to him with narrowed eyes. "What about that breakfast sandwich you took from the Wawa down the block?"

"That was an accident!" Timothy protests.

While the two of them bicker about the semantics of what counts as stealing, I lower my own thumb into my palm. I take a quick, discreet sip of my drink and hope none of them will notice. The alcohol burns the second it touches my tongue—the fizz combined with the Bacardi as electric as battery acid. I took the smallest sip I possibly could, but it still travels down my throat like tar, settling at the pit of my stomach.

After I've white-knuckled my way through the sip, I shake myself off to find Timothy staring right at me, his mouth open in silent shock. "Oh shit," he says over a chuckle, just loud enough to get the others attention.

I can feel the heat of their eyes on me within seconds—everyone in the tub suddenly staring at the four fingers I'm holding up against my chest. I resist the urge to shove my hand beneath the water to avoid explaining the what and the why. Looking at all their shocked faces, though, part of me does feel a bit of a thrill. I like that I've surprised them. That I've proven there's more to me than my family's story. That I can be someone worthy of being in their circle, be the regular teenage girl I've always wanted to be.

Kiki shakes her head in disbelief. "No way," she says as if the thought of me stealing something is as likely as me heading to the moon.

Kai turns to me with a raised brow that I'm not sure how to interpret. Whether it's curious, impressed, or concerned. "Seriously?"

"It was just something small. A pack of gum," I say quickly, going with the first lie I can think of. I won't let the truth ruin the moment that brought us here—the dress I hoped would make him see me in a new light.

"Good for you." Carla raises her cup to me in a salute before taking a sip of her drink and lowering her index finger, now down to just three fingers. She takes her time thinking through her options, tapping the fingers she has left standing against the bare expanse of her collarbone. "Never have I ever . . . sent a nude from school."

Timothy snorts lazily before bringing another finger down—the thought of him in any state of undress, but especially at school, makes me shudder. Beside me I can feel Kai stiffen uncomfortably, but he doesn't put a finger down. An unexpected pressure eases in my chest. I'm not exactly sure what Kai's romantic history is. For all I know he's dated dozens of girls since he started at Millcreek. Plenty of girls have been interested, that I know for sure. And just because I never saw him holding hands in the halls or the cafeteria with someone doesn't mean that he didn't have someone behind closed doors. He's already managed to keep us—whatever it is we are—a secret this entire time.

But if he didn't put a finger down, then why does he look like he has something to hide?

Timothy's mouth parts into an O like it did earlier for me. A wordless gasp. "Oh sh—"

"Shut up," Kiki interrupts before he can finish. She shoves her hand beneath the water, but through the blur I can see she's put another finger down.

"Naughty girl, Ki," Carla teases with a smirk.

Kiki splashes in Carla's direction, earning a surprisingly high-pitched scream from Timothy, while Kai buries his face in his hands.

"Can we please never talk about my sister and nudes at the same time ever again?" he pleads, peeking through his fingertips at Carla who shrugs in agreement.

Silence settles over us and it's not until the others start to peek over at me that I realize it's my turn. I inhale sharply as my brain kicks into overdrive, trying to sort through the dozens of things I haven't done. I would've said *had alcohol* if it weren't for the sip I took seconds earlier. Besides a few sips of Mami's wine or Papi's Coronas over the years, which I don't count, it's the first time I've been any sort of reckless when it comes to alcohol.

"I . . ." I bite back a groan as I realize I've already screwed up, getting the format of the question wrong. "Never have I ever kissed somebody."

Thanks to the panic of screwing up before I'd even begun, I blurted out the first thing that came to mind. Unfortunately, it was the most embarrassing confession I could have made. Maybe with a different crowd it wouldn't have seemed so unusual, but this is the social elite. The types of people whose relationships are front page news. Kissing is child's play to them. A dozen kisses under their belts by freshman year. Surprisingly, though, instead of being met with unanimous pity or laughter, I'm graced with an array of reactions.

"Awwww," Carla coos before lowering one of her fingers and taking a sip, looking at me like she wants to pinch my cheeks.

Beside her, Timothy mumbles something under his breath before taking a sip of his drink—now down to just two fingers.

"My mom's really strict," I say quickly, doing my best to cover up my pathetic lack of a love life. Mentioning Mami makes me wince, as if I might summon her by just saying her name. I bite my tongue before I can keep rambling. About all the slumber parties I bailed on. All the friend groups I faded to the background of. All the horrible things Mami dealt with when she was my age—all the things she's trying to save me from.

I almost don't have the strength to look at Kai, avoiding facing him until I feel him shift closer to me. "You really haven't kissed anyone?" he whispers, so close his knee bumps against mine. The contact is dulled by the weightlessness of the water, but doesn't dampen the spark.

I shrug, my cheeks as warm as the water bubbling around us. "Guess I never found the right person," I mumble.

Kai's lips part, but he doesn't say anything. His brows are arched, as if in confusion or surprise. And I'm not sure if I should be flattered or worried. Or if this changes what he thinks about me—and whether it's for the better, or for worse.

Before I can lose myself to that worry, Kiki snaps her fingers at Kai to get the game back on track. "Let's go, lover boy. It's your turn."

Kai quickly turns toward Kiki until he's no longer leaning into me. "Never have I ever been an annoying younger sister," he shoots back, eyes narrowed to slits.

Kiki responds with a buzzer sound and a thumbs-down. "Try again. And you're not older."

"Ten minutes still makes me older," he taunts before giving in with a shrug. "Never have I ever cut class."

"Goody Two-shoes," Kiki mutters after her sip.

"Says Ms. I've Never Gotten a Detention," he snaps back.

"Yeah, because I know how to break the rules *without* getting caught."

Kai rolls his eyes so intensely I briefly wonder if Mami's warning to me and Joel that our eyes would get stuck forever could come true. "Are you done gloating, or are you gonna go?"

Kiki takes her time thinking of a reply. She hums and taps her perfectly manicured coffin-shaped nails against her plastic cup. Makes us all wait until Timothy starts to loll his head around in bored impatience. Her eyes lock somewhere in Carla and Timothy's direction—the two of them too close together for me to tell which one of them she's looking at as the corner of her lips tug into a devilish smirk. "Never have I ever cheated on someone."

Both Carla and Timothy stiffen. When they move, it's apart from each other. Carla slips out from beneath Timothy's arm while he shoves his fist beneath the water now that he doesn't have any fingers left to hold up.

“Fuck you, Kiki,” he mutters before downing the last of his drink.

Kai looks as though he’s going to protest Timothy telling off his sister, but Kiki doesn’t seem to mind at all. In fact, she looks perfectly pleased as she crosses her arms. Carla doesn’t meet her gaze as she finishes her own drink and tosses the cup aside before shoving her hands beneath her armpits.

Neither Kai nor I dare to say anything as the others finally look at one another. Timothy glaring at Kiki, and Kiki smirking at Carla, and Carla and Timothy looking at each other with a strange intensity that makes the water feel electrically charged. Kai and I share our own confused look while the others wage their silent war with each other. He shrugs his shoulders subtly, as lost as I am. Even without context, it’s obvious something is going on. Something I *definitely* don’t want to be a part of.

13

After Timothy excuses himself from the tub to pour himself another drink, the casual, teasing vibe of the party is back as if nothing happened. Kiki and Carla smile at one another like they didn't look like were about to tear each other apart seconds earlier.

Timothy returns and slides in on Carla's right instead of her left this time. Which puts him directly next to me. He stays silent as we play another round of Never Have I Ever. I brace myself for him to slide in closer to me, or worse—for his hand to disappear beneath the water to somewhere he knows it shouldn't be—but he keeps his attention focused on Carla and the game.

After two more rounds of increasingly more specific things, it's down to me, Kai, and Carla.

"I thought you were on my team," Kai grumbles as he lets his hand fall into the water with a plop. Looks like having been to Europe was his downfall.

"There are no teams, just winners," I reply with a teasing smile, surprised at my own boldness—either from the rush of being here tonight with him, or the rum. Most likely a combination of both.

Kiki, who struck out shortly after Timothy, raises a brow in surprise. "That's the spirit," she says, and I can't help but beam at the small sliver of her approval.

Carla, on the other hand, doesn't seem as entertained. Down to just one finger while I still have four, we both know who's most likely going to take the game. With it now being her turn, though, she can at least go down swinging.

"Never have I ever . . ." She pauses, and I can see the moment the idea comes to her. Watch as her eyes light up with a wicked thrill. "Had a dad who was a murderer."

It's as if all the air has been sucked out of me. The silence weighs so heavy, even the hot tub's jets seem to simmer down, the cicadas in the surrounding woods hushing. I can't move, can't even so much as blink as my vision tunnels—focused on Carla's sneering smile. Dozens of thoughts whip through my mind at lightning speed, all of them fighting for dominance. I want to push her. Make her pay. I want to beg her for forgiveness for a crime I didn't commit. I want to scream.

More than anything, I want to disappear.

"What the fuck, Carla?!" Kai shouts loud enough to break me from my daze. He stands up out of the water, looking as though he's going to lunge at her until Kiki grabs him by the wrist. "That's not cool."

"It's not like it's a secret," Carla protests casually as she gestures toward me like I'm a zoo animal. Like she didn't poke at the rawest part of me—all for the sake of winning a stupid drinking game.

It may not be a secret, but that doesn't mean she knows anything about me, or Papi, or our family. She has no idea who we are. Or what we're capable of.

"Her dad probably didn't even do it, though," Timothy says suddenly, the statement so jarring that everyone—me included—whips around to face him. "Those guys were assholes."

I swallow down a gulp, feeling more lightheaded than ever. He's right, but it's not something anyone ever says out loud. In death, those boys were forgiven of all the things they'd done. How they broke our family in ways we didn't know were possible.

People often forget about those details. That there was more to the story than what happened that afternoon because Coach Kills Two of His Star Players makes a better headline. Hardly anyone mentions the months leading up to it. The anti-bullying seminars we were forced to sit through month after month and the school-sponsored psychologists that assured us their doors were open but never did anything to help those who really needed it. They forgot all about my brother because something darker came along to take his place.

"Timothy," Carla replies in warning, bitter and biting as ice. It was bold enough for Timothy to say what everyone thought out loud, but especially in front of her. The mourning ex-girlfriend.

Timothy shakes his head lazily, completely unfazed by Carla's glare. "Please, you said it yourself. The guy was a dick."

The truth of what happened between Carla and Jose, the king and queen of Millcreek High, isn't public knowledge like the rest of her breakups. Maybe it was at one time, but anything unkind people had to say about Jose Perez is long buried with him. But it's not surprising that they didn't last long. He was a senior dating a freshman—that alone painted an ugly picture.

"That doesn't mean he deserved to die," Carla snaps back,

her cheeks flushed just a few shades lighter than her red bikini. I'm not sure if the frantic edge to her tone is rage or defensiveness.

"That's not what I meant," Timothy says, rolling his eyes. "They just did a lot of shitty stuff. Like *a lot*. The whole goddamn soccer team hated them. Danny was on the football team my freshman year, and he made our lives hell before getting kicked off." He looks around at us as if we'll all jump to agree with him—though he spends extra time lingering on me. I don't give him the satisfaction of any kind of response. Not a blink or a twitch of a smile or even a breath. He flushes when he looks away from me, sober enough to realize he put his foot in his mouth but not enough to shut up while he's ahead. "Lots of people could've wanted them dead."

Timothy holds his hands up as he leans up against the wall of the hot tub. "I'm just saying, the story seems a little too convenient."

His theory isn't the first I've heard like it, and probably won't be the last. While it's easy to feel like the entire world is against us, there are some people who believe Papi is innocent. Usually, I found comfort in knowing that there were people out there who saw to the core of Papi's heart—who knew as well as I did that he was good and kind and gentle. But this is different. Timothy doesn't believe in Papi. He just hates those boys for hurting him like they did us. Even if he believes that Papi was—*is*—innocent, he's not any better than the others. He doesn't care about the truth, or about us, or about who we really are. All he wants is to mold us into exactly what he needs us to be. Just so we can fit his version of the story.

As much as I hate to admit it, Carla is right. No matter what, those boys didn't deserve to die. They deserved consequences, but not ones that cost them their lives. And I've always wished I could say that out loud.

With Timothy resting his case, no one bothers to argue with him. No one tries to change the topic either, the air too loaded with tension for us to act like everything is okay. Suddenly, I'm warm all over with the urge to be sick. I grip the edge of the hot tub, prepared to make a bolt for the bathroom, but just as I lift myself out of the water there's a pop somewhere in the distance. I swear I see a spark somewhere between the trees, moments before the world goes black.

EXHIBIT G: COMPLAINT FILED BY JOEL SOTO WITH THE MILLCREEK HIGH SCHOOL ADMINISTRATION

STUDENT COMPLAINT #Q39A

Name: Joel Soto
Year: 11
Student ID: 107A
File Date: October 9

By request of his father, Millcreek High soccer coach David Soto, Joel Soto made an appointment with counselor Jessica Finn. While initially reluctant to open up, Soto eventually disclosed that he'd been the victim of ongoing bullying by fellow juniors Jose Perez and Danny Bauer. Said bullying was alleged to include name calling (including various slurs about Soto's sexuality), and several instances of physical abuse (punching, kicking, and slapping being explicitly named). Following his session with Mrs. Finn, Soto expressed interest in pursuing action against Perez and Bauer.

A formal investigation was conducted, including reviewing camera footage from the vicinity of the team locker room, as well as interviewing Soto, Perez, and Bauer's teammates. No evidence was found to support Soto's claims. Unless new evidence is presented, this case will be considered closed on November 27.

14

Screams rip through the silence and water splashes onto me but all I can make out are the vague outlines of bodies scrambling to make their way to safety in the pitch-black night. Without any light to guide us, it's pure madness. A frantic free-for-all as arms and elbows shove into me so roughly I'm knocked beneath the water before I can ever stand up. Warmth burns my cheeks and water clogs my throat, my sinuses, my everything as I push myself back to the surface as quickly as I can. The whiplash of the slight chill against my too-warm skin stings as harsh as a bruise as I rub my eyes in a desperate attempt to get them to adjust to the dark faster.

"Everyone calm down!" Kai's voice interjects from somewhere over my shoulder. When I turn around, my vision has cleared enough for me to see the glimmer of one of his earrings. "A fuse probably blew. I'll go check it out."

Behind me, someone whimpers.

"Does anyone have their phone?" Kai asks, his voice steady but uneven, like he's barely keeping it together.

"Mine's upstairs," I offer up when no one else does. There should still be plenty of battery since I turned it off as soon as I got here, but getting all the way upstairs without any light is its own challenge.

"I think I left mine on the table," Kiki finally says, sounding unusually distant. Maybe she was able to make it out of the tub without breaking a bone in the process.

No one dares move a muscle or make a sound as Kai roots through the dark for the table. The wood of the deck creaks beneath his slow, careful footsteps. Hitched gasps ring out when we hear part of him collide with something solid enough to make him hiss. "I'm okay," he reassures us. Based on the silence, he must take his time to work through the pain before moving again.

I crane my neck until I can make out the sound of his hand gently patting the table on the opposite end of the deck, searching for Kiki's phone. My muscles begin to ache from the strain when a piercing light shines directly at me. I wrench my eyes shut and back away like a vampire from the sun, stars blooming behind my closed lids.

"Shit, sorry," Kai mumbles before adjusting his grip, pointing the phone's flashlight toward the floor instead.

It's enough light for me to make out the shape of him—how his hands are trembling. How he's hunched in on himself—either from the cold, or to make himself feel smaller. A less visible target. A stark contrast to the calm confidence he'd put on when he addressed us.

Carefully, he shines the light just below the hot tub and holds his hand out toward me. With his help I'm able to get out of the water and join Kiki on the edge of the deck, just a few feet from the sliding door. He begrudgingly does the same for Carla and Timothy, waiting until everyone is safely out of the tub to point the flashlight toward the sky, bathing all of us in the dim but harsh light.

"We should have flashlights in one of the kitchen drawers.

They'll work better than our phones," he says calmly, looking at me, Carla, and Kiki. "And I'll need help getting the ladder out from the garage." This time, he looks pointedly at Timothy.

It takes several seconds for Timothy to pick up on Kai's unsaid request, blinking at us in confusion before looking back at Kai with wide, panicked eyes. "Why does it have to be me?" he squeaks out—a sound I'd find amusing if my heart wasn't still pounding so hard I can feel it vibrating through my entire body.

"Because you're the boys," Carla snaps as if it's obvious. "And boys never die first in horror movies."

Whether or not that's true, it's a solid enough argument for Timothy to reluctantly give in. "Fine," he mutters, pulling on his sneakers before walking to the edge of the deck, where a small staircase leads out to the back of the cabin. "Lead the way."

Left to fend for ourselves, Kiki, Carla, and I carefully make our way back into the cabin, feeling our way along the edges of the deck until we're able to make it to the door. As soon as the boys turn the corner, we're left in the same darkness we started with. Instantly, I regret not asking Kai to stay and help us find the flashlights before he went to check out the fuse. If Kiki and Carla have the same thought, they don't say it out loud—either because they're too proud, or too scared to go back outside and call for help that might not come. You don't have to watch many horror movies to know that that's a rookie mistake. The kind that, if this were more than just a blown fuse, could cost us more than we could ever imagine. I shudder at the thought, frozen in place as soon as the door to the deck slides shut behind me.

Maybe it's the horror movie still fresh in my mind, but the cabin seems a lot more menacing now than it did when we first arrived.

Thankfully, Kiki knows the layout well enough that she walks ahead of us with confidence, not needing to feel along the walls to find her way through the space. Beside me, Carla chooses to linger by the door too. Outside may have felt more dangerous, but at least we had the moon for comfort. It wasn't much, but inside we don't even have so much as the glowing clock on the microwave to guide us.

The room is silent except for the sound of Kiki's soft footsteps. My skin prickles when the footsteps stop—Kiki is far away enough that she's disappeared completely into the void of darkness, nothing left of her but the lingering scent of her perfume. Carla begins tapping her foot impatiently. Between the irregular tapping I hear the flick of a light switch. Once, twice, then a rapid flutter, but nothing changes.

"It doesn't work," Kiki says with a grunt. I don't need to see her to picture the annoyance and anger that must be written all over her.

"Of course it doesn't work," Carla snaps, and lets out a huff of air before returning to tapping her foot.

Before I can decide whether it's worth following the sound of Kiki's voice and walking toward the kitchen, I'm startled by a clattering sound that feels as loud as thunder. Kiki rustling through the kitchen drawers. After several seconds of muttered curses to herself, Kiki lets out a nervous laugh before light fills the room. Following her brother's lead, Kiki points the flashlight she's found toward the ceiling, bathing the room in enough light for me and Carla to rush over to her in the kitchen.

"Here." She tosses me another flashlight, which I narrowly catch. It's heavier than I expect it to be and powerful enough to make me wince when I peek at the beam head-on. Kiki points hers toward the staircase. "I think we have some candles in the attic." She heads for the stairs but pauses and turns to look at Carla when she doesn't follow.

"I'm not going to the attic," Carla protests, crossing her arms firmly. "That shit's creepy in the daytime."

Kiki glares at her best friend, but I can sense something unsaid passing between the two of them. Communicating in a wordless language that only they know, not unlike when we were in the hot tub. The heat of Kiki's gaze is enough to make me shift uncomfortably. I'm considering walking away, wondering if I should give them some privacy, when Carla finally gives in with a groan. She stomps across the room and follows Kiki up the stairs.

I linger in the kitchen after they disappear from view. Above me I can hear the creak of their footsteps along the carpeted second-floor hallway and the hum of a whispered conversation, but soon I'm plunged into absolute silence. Again.

Alone and unsure what to do, I try to make myself useful. I open more drawers and cabinets, looking for anything else we could use as a light source. I have no clue what goes into fixing a fuse box, but I gather all the tools I find on the kitchen counter in case Kai might need them. I keep expecting to hear more signs of Kiki and Carla hovering above me, or maybe Kai and Timothy coming back from outside, but there's no sign of life other than my own. No footsteps. No murmurs.

Until a sudden, thundering crash.

The floor trembles and the frames on the staircase rattle. On instinct I let out a scream, only to clamp my hand around my mouth to muffle it. As if I'm worried about someone finding me, even though I know I'm all alone.

I press myself as far up against the wall as I can, scanning my flashlight across the room for any signs of what could've made the noise. Nothing is out of place except for the dust floating through the air. Hesitantly, I take a step toward the stairs. Wait. Listen for any cries for help from Kiki or Carla. But it's so quiet that if my heart wasn't pounding out of my chest, I might think I'd made up the sound entirely.

Maybe it came from outside, I tell myself as I give the room one more sweep with the flashlight. Nothing emerges from behind the couch or the trees gently swaying in the breeze outside. I'm still alone.

Once I'm sure nothing is lurking in the shadows to come get me, I take another step toward the stairs. My phone is still upstairs in my bag, and we could use another light source. Even if it means braving the dark alone—and whatever notifications may be waiting for me. I'm careful to keep my steps as light as possible in case Kiki or Carla couldn't cry for help because something—or someone—made sure they couldn't. It's a silly, outlandish thought, but we've already made one rookie mistake by splitting up, and I don't plan to make another.

At the landing, I'm able to make out the outline of the attic door in the ceiling. Completely sealed shut. My brows furrow in confusion when hushed whispers suddenly catch my attention.

I switch off my flashlight before I reach the top step, just in case, moving as quietly as I possibly can. My breath hitches when I notice a strip of light coming from an open door. I press myself into the shadows and crane my neck toward the voices.

"It wasn't funny," Kiki says just loud enough for me to make out.

My entire body stiffens as I realize my mistake. Of course it wasn't an intruder—how would they have gotten into the cabin without us noticing? Biting my lip, I push myself farther into the dark and away from the door as I map out an escape plan. I could try to make a break for the stairs, but that runs the risk of them noticing me. And there's no way to explain why I came up just to turn back around.

Going past them isn't an option either, with their door wide open. Based on the light spilling out of the room they must have their flashlight sitting on some piece of furniture. Sure, I still need my phone, but that can at least wait until I don't look like I'm eavesdropping on their conversation.

"It was a joke, Ki," Carla protests, sounding exasperated and farther away. "And *you're* the one who took it too far."

I'm not sure why I do it. Why I linger when I know I should leave. Maybe it's because I'm not any better than the kids at our school—that I'm as desperate for gossip as everyone who followed my father's trial like it was the latest hit TV show. Or, maybe, it's because of the knot that formed in my stomach as soon as I heard Kiki's voice. The sinking feeling that they might be talking about me.

Kiki scoffs, her footsteps urgent and steady and her shadow passing in and out of the flashlight's beam with a startling consistency. She must be pacing. "Right, because you have no idea that Timothy's been cheating on you since day one."

"That's not what I meant."

Kiki's shadow stills. Slowly, her crossed arms fall to her sides. "Then what did you mean?"

"I think you know . . ." Carla's voice is so low I almost can't make out her response. There's a strangely playful edge to her tone—I can almost picture the smirk tugging at the corner of her lips as she says it.

By now it's clear they're not talking about me. I should leave before I hear something I shouldn't, but I don't move. And neither does Kiki, her shadow finally standing still.

Kiki doesn't respond for so long my spine starts to ache from the way I've arched against the wall to hear more clearly. I'm not sure if they're ignoring each other or having another one of their stare offs, but footsteps break the tension between them. In the flashlight's glow I watch Kiki's and Carla's shadows meet each other halfway. They stall in front of each other, holding for a blink-and-you'll-miss-it moment before they collide. Fingers tangling in each other's hair and clutching each other's waists as their mouths crash together. Even from the hallway I can feel the hunger as they move against each other—the wet sounds of hurried kisses and quiet moans as they break from each other's mouths to explore jaws and necks and the shells of their ears. Their movements so frantic and their bodies pressed so tightly together that I can't tell whose shadow is whose anymore.

Grabbing my flashlight off the ground, I scramble up as quickly and quietly as I can—the spell of wanting to know more finally broken. The carpet pads my footsteps, and Kiki and Carla are thankfully too wrapped up in one another to see the shadow of my hair whip by as I run past the door. I head for my bedroom at the end of the hall as fast as I dare. I've already intruded more than I should have, and the faster I leave them alone, the better.

Just as I'm about to reach for the knob, a crash stops me in my tracks. Just like before, I let out a choked sound of surprise, my body acting on pure adrenaline and fear. Immediately, I clamp my hand around my mouth again, as I turn around to check for the source of the noise.

"C'mon, those things cost like a hundred bucks," Kiki complains, and I watch her shadow pick something up off the floor. A doll whose face has been shattered, based on the outline of their shadows.

But Carla doesn't respond, instead, her shadow grows bigger as she inches toward the door. "Did you hear that?" she whispers, sending my heart straight into the pit of my stomach.

My hand stiffens where it's clamped around the doorknob, tightening its grip until my fingers start to ache. Opening the door means making more noise—drawing more attention. So I stay as still as I possibly can, hoping they won't notice me frozen in the shadowed hallway. An animal hiding from its predator.

Still as I manage to be, I know I'm caught the second Carla steps out into the hallway. Before I can turn the knob and throw the door open, she's sprinted over, yanking me back by the arm. Her grip tight enough to make me yelp.

"What the fuck are you doing?" she shouts so close to my ear I wince.

"I thought—"

"Did you see anything?" Kiki interrupts before I can finish explaining myself.

I don't answer immediately, unsure whether telling the truth is the right move or not. What they do behind Carla's boyfriend's back isn't any of my business. I'm already regretting coming up here in the first place—for lingering when I know I shouldn't have.

But Kiki doesn't give me time to decide whether it's worth being honest with her. She stomps toward me with enough power to make the ground beneath us shake. We're nearly pressed chest to chest and nose to nose when she finally stops, radiating enough heat to light a dozen furnaces.

"Whatever you saw, forget it." Her tone makes it clear it's more than just a command—it's a warning. Somehow, she leans even closer, until I can smell the tequila on her breath. See the smudge of Carla's cherry-red lip-gloss on her bottom lip. "You never should've been here in the first place," she says through gritted teeth. "Kai may have brought you in, but I will happily take you out."

I'm too panicked to reply, so I nod until she seems satisfied. Hold my breath until she finally backs away from me.

Her eyes are narrowed to slits, watching me over her shoulder as she grabs Carla by the arm and drags her back to their bedroom. Before I can even let out the breath I was holding, Kiki slams the door behind her, the force of it so intense it knocks me back. As soon as they're behind a closed door, I don't hesitate like I did before. This time, I run.

15

I'm not sure what to do once I close the door to my room. Hide is my first instinct, but what's the point in that when I've already been caught? All I want is to dig myself into a hole or find some other way to disappear. Anything that'll take away the guilt and panic gnawing inside me. All the feelings I'd plugged up on the drive up here—about Mami, about sneaking out, about myself—come bubbling back to the surface.

Now, I'm willing to be honest with myself. To confess that I'm barely keeping my head above water—that I'm so out of my element here that I might as well be on a different planet. Even the few moments spent with Kai can't outshine the fear pulsing through me. My skin still burns where Carla yanked me. I can still feel the vibration of Kiki's stomps as she closed the distance between us—feel the chill from the iciness of her voice.

I don't belong here. And it was a mistake ever thinking that I could.

It's too late now for me to go home tonight, though, so I focus on what I came up here for in the first place. I amble over to the edge of the bed and find my phone buried at the bottom of my bag. The extra light source will be helpful, but my thumb hesitates over the power button.

Worst-case scenario, Mami realized I was missing and my

phone will be flooded with calls and texts from her the second I power it back on. While the thought of facing Carla and Kiki again makes me feel like I'd be walking directly into the sun, facing Mami feels just as terrifying.

It might soften the blow—talking to her over the phone instead of in person. Explaining why I left and how sorry I am. I can only imagine the grounding she'll hit me with once I'm home on Sunday. Not that it really matters—I never went anywhere to begin with. But I know I won't call her either way. Because the truth is: I don't want to admit defeat. Not to her. Admitting it to myself is one thing, but telling Mami she was right to be so protective is something else entirely. It means even less freedom, for me and for Mikey. A confirmation that her worst fears were founded in truth: that when we stray, we get hurt. That it's not worth having friends when our family are the only people we can trust.

Kai may have felt like my one shot at a normal teenage life. But the world is bigger than Millcreek. There's no money for me to go to college, but I don't need an education to start somewhere new. Somewhere far away where no one knows my name or thinks they know my story. I know after this weekend Mami will be reluctant to ever let me leave the house again, but at least there's a chance she'd let me leave someday. Once I've learned my lesson.

But not if she knows she was right.

The best thing I can hope for is that Kai and Timothy will get the lights back on and I can white-knuckle my way through the rest of the weekend. Avoid giving Kiki and Carla more reasons to be upset with me while I keep their secret.

I wince from the harsh white light of the phone coming to life. I'm not sure whether to be relieved or concerned when I'm not met with a flurry of messages. My phone is as barren as a desert most days, and tonight is no exception. Either Mami hasn't realized I've gone yet, or she has and just can't reach me thanks to the glaring NO SERVICE message in the upper right-hand corner of the screen.

Well, even if I wanted to bail it doesn't look like I could escape anytime soon.

After flicking on the flashlight, I hesitate on my home screen. I stare at the red notification over the phone icon. The voicemail Mikey left earlier. Should I listen? I scan the room like the answer might be written on the eggshell-white walls, but ultimately I give in to my curiosity.

It can't be anything major if he didn't keep calling and texting. Especially if Mami didn't follow up with calls of her own. It's probably just another warning to be back on time, or a threat to hold this over my head unless I do his homework for a week. I've nearly convinced myself that I should just delete the voicemail when the message begins to play. The volume so unexpectedly loud it makes me drop my phone.

But the speaker doesn't have to be pressed to my ear for me to hear the panic in Mikey's voice. I don't even pick it back up as I kneel down on the carpet beside the phone, his voice—and his fear—coming through loud and clear.

He's rambling too quickly for me to catch what he's saying at first—something about trouble—only to trail off for so long I wonder if he forgot to hang up the phone. But there's no mistaking what he says when his voice does come back—low and desperate and as afraid as the night those boys died.

You're not safe there.

16

All my fear about facing Kiki and Carla comes rushing back as I listen to Mikey's voicemail again. If they had something planned, they would have done it by now, right? Or were they waiting to get me away from Kai? To get me alone—like I am now?

But that's Mami talking. The paranoia she instilled in me is hard to shake. Her voice in my head tells me to lock the door and not leave until the lights come back on, but the rational side of my brain tells me to find Kai. To ask him if he has any idea what Mikey may have meant.

Without giving myself the chance to overthink it, I bolt out of the room and back downstairs as quickly as my legs will carry me. The door to Kiki and Carla's room is closed, and I hope they don't hear me pass by.

The living room is colder than I remember it being just a few minutes earlier. A chill creeps down my spine as I reach the bottom of the stairs—stopping so quickly I nearly trip over myself as I realize the reason for the cold.

The sliding door is open.

Using my phone flashlight, I quickly scan the room for any sign of an intruder, but it seems empty. There are no damp footprints on the ground, no indents on the couch, nothing obviously out of place. No shadows lurking in corners or flashes of movement out of the corner of my eye.

Still, I stay on guard.

"Hello?" I call out, but no one answers. I take a cautious step forward, shining the flashlight across the room once again. "Kai?"

I brace myself for Kai's voice, his laugh teasing me for being so on edge, but still nothing. Moving on instinct, I reach out for the first sturdy thing I can find—a decorative vase perched on the mantel beside me. It's heavy enough to do some damage if I slam it over someone's head, but not so heavy that I struggle to carry it with me.

I turn around and scan the kitchen. I'm sure there are knives somewhere in the dozens of drawers and cabinets, but I'm not sure I trust myself with something that dangerous. I'd probably wind up hurting myself before I could hurt a potential intruder.

And that's assuming this isn't all an elaborate prank.

Edging toward the open sliding door, I tell myself that's all this is. The "something" Mikey said they had planned. A cruel joke—planned by either Kiki or Carla or Timothy, or maybe even Kai—to scare the hell out of me. While I might be safer with a knife, they wouldn't be. With my reputation, that's the last thing I need. Ammo for them to tell the entire school that the murderer's daughter pulled a knife on them in the woods.

I swallow hard and creep to the edge of the room, peering out the sliding door for any signs of life. Steam rises out of the powered down hot tub, the water now still without the jets at full blast. A plastic cup knocked on its side dances along the edge of the table, threatening to tip over onto the ground any second. And then I see it, quick as a flash.

Something moving through the trees.

I'd swear it was my imagination if I hadn't heard it too. The crunch of dried leaves and snapped twigs. I scan my flashlight across the horizon but can't see anything. Don't spot any footprints in the mud at the edge of the tree line. Maybe it was an animal. A deer, or maybe something else. I kick myself for not paying better attention in bio—to what animals might lurk in the woods on the edge of Millcreek.

In a probably foolish move, I step outside.

"Kai?" I call out again, louder this time. If there *is* something out there, I want to make sure he's safe. Call him back inside where at least we can stick together.

Something rustles in the trees when I take another step out onto the deck. I point my flashlight directly at it and tighten my grip on the vase, prepared to lob it if I have to. A branch twitches, shaking dead leaves onto the ground but nothing comes out of the shadows.

"Hey."

The scream I let out could wake the dead. There are no neighbors within visible distance, but I wouldn't be surprised if the closest one still heard my shout. I nearly leap out of my skin at the sight of Timothy, hands held high in the air as he backs away from me as if burned.

"Jesus, it's just me," he reassures, but it's too late. The vase slips out of my hands when I jump back in surprise, shattering the second it hits the ground. Shards of glass scatter across the deck, most big enough to avoid but some so small it would be impossible to spot them even during the day.

"Where's Kai?" I ask instantly, holding my phone close to my chest now that my weapon is gone.

Suddenly, I regret not changing out of my swimsuit before I headed back downstairs. An untouched stack of fresh towels is sitting on the table just a few feet away, but I don't dare move an inch. Without shoes or flip-flops on I'm practically guaranteed to get a piece of glass wedged in my foot if I move.

Timothy must catch my eyes lingering on the towels. I recognize Kiki's hot pink phone case as he holds the flashlight up and gingerly crosses the deck toward the table. Last I checked, Kai was the one who had Kiki's phone. The thought of Timothy taking it from Kai makes me worry, but I can't do anything, trapped by the ring of broken glass. I can hear the shards crunching beneath his sneakers, but if they pierce through the soles he doesn't seem to notice. Once he's made it to the table, he tosses me a towel before wrapping one around his own shoulders. I quickly wrap mine around my torso but don't feel any less exposed when he saunters back to me with a glint in his eyes that I don't trust.

"He's in the middle of doing some rewiring shit. Asked me to grab him some tweezers from the bathroom cabinet." He wiggles the phone, an explanation for how he got it.

It takes me a moment to realize what he's talking about, completely forgetting that I'd asked him about Kai. The reassurance that he's just on the other side of the cabin sets me at ease, but I know better than to let my guard down. Clutching the knot of the towel tight, I give him a tightlipped smile and gesture toward the open sliding door. "Well, I won't stop you."

Timothy lets out a quiet laugh that I'm not sure how to interpret—whether it's meant at my expense or not. Either way, he turns around and heads for the door. But my breath hitches as he walks away, waiting until he's fully out of view to breathe out again. Sure enough, he stops at the entryway, pausing for a moment before flipping around. "I'm sorry for what Carla said."

"Wh—" The shock of the apology catches me so off guard I almost step out of my protective ring and toward the shattered glass. I shake my head and the apology off. "It's fine."

"She's such a bitch sometimes," he says so casually you'd never think he was talking about his girlfriend.

The harshness of it stings like a slap. He wasn't talking about me, and I'm by no means Carla's number one fan, but the way he talks about someone he supposedly loves sits uncomfortably in my gut. And as much as I don't like Carla, she's not wrong to be upset at the way he talked about her ex. Or the way she feels about me. I may not have been the one who murdered Jose, but we rarely point our anger at the person who deserves it most. I'm the closest thing she has to Papi, so I'm her target.

Does he know about her and Kiki? I wonder, biting down on my lip before I can give in to my curiosity and ask. Clearly his and Carla's relationship is a special kind of toxic. Even if I hadn't seen his girlfriend and Kiki hooking up a few minutes earlier, that much was obvious from the minute they both essentially confessed to cheating on each other during Never Have I Ever.

Suddenly, I see the game in a new, voyeuristic light. The knowing glances between Kiki and Carla feel even more loaded now. The tension between Carla and Timothy. They'd seemed like every other PDA-obsessed teenage couple. Was that all just a show for the rest of us? Or for each other?

Timothy sighs and runs a hand through his thick brown hair, dragging it down along the edge of his defined jaw. "Don't listen to anything she says," he continues, not picking up on my obvious discomfort. He takes a step toward me. Then another, and another, until he's uncomfortably close to invading my space again. He's tall enough that he has to lean down slightly to look me in the eyes—his so piercing that if I were a different girl, the weakness in my knees might be for all the right reasons. "Her opinion doesn't matter."

And yours does? I think bitterly but would never say out loud. He has me exactly where he wants me—pinned in place and surrounded by an ocean of broken glass. No matter what I do—run away or stay—I'm going to get hurt.

"It's n—"

I'm not sure how I'm going to finish that sentence—what I could possibly say to make him back away—but he doesn't give me the chance. Before the words can tumble out of my mouth, he has his on my mine, cutting me short like I've come unplugged. His lips are as cold as his hands. Damp all over like he's still drying off from the hot tub with pruned fingertips. Despite the cold, his touch is urgent, firm as he cups my cheek with enough force to hold me in place and kiss me as hard as he wants. It's rough and teeth and the taste of tequila and too fast and too much.

Everything about it is wrong, wrong, wrong. From the way his thumb digs into the curve of my jaw tight enough to leave the wrong kind of bruise in the morning. From the way he reaches for the small of my back, clothed by the towel but still too close. From the earthy smell of smoke and cherries still clinging to his skin.

When I snuck out through my window, this is what I'd hoped for: A boy I never imagined would ever want to kiss me in the dim glow of the moonlight. But all of those dreams turn as sour as the taste on Timothy's tongue. All at once Mami's voice comes swirling back. Warning me that I should've never left home. Warning me that they'll never see me as equal.

Warning me that they'll only ever see me as something they can hurt.

That sadness morphs into something darker the tighter he holds me. An emotion as boiling hot as the water from the tub, threatening to spill over and burn anyone in its path. New strength flows through me, but I'm too afraid of what it might mean to act on it. How easy it would be to grab one of the glass shards once he lets me go and push it straight into his heart. To make him pay for all the ways he hurt me.

"What the fuck, man?!" Kai's voice cuts in just in time, before those dangerous thoughts can take over.

In almost slow motion, I find the strength to push Timothy away but not without giving up some of my balance. I shove him off me with all the fight I have left, but he's sturdy enough to send me wobbling back. Pain slices through me the exact moment the glass pierces my foot—red-hot and blinding as I struggle to find a way to stay balanced and still keep Timothy far away.

I don't even have time to register Kai's presence—that he saw what happened between us. All I hear is an "oof" as Timothy smacks against the deck railing and suddenly Kai is beside me, readying to kneel on the ground but stalling when he sees the glass.

"Hey, it's just me," he whispers, and it's only then that I hear the sobs. Primal and gut-wrenching and, somehow, coming from me. Tears roll down my cheeks, my fingers shaking as I go to reach out for him for balance but find myself pulling away instead.

Because I'm afraid. Of him. Of touch.

And maybe deep down somewhere, of myself.

In just a few seconds Timothy managed to take away my

trust. A single unwanted kiss has cut straight through me, draining me of all my hope and faith that good things would eventually find me. For a fleeting moment, I consider that Mami may have been right. I should never trust anyone.

Even Kai.

"We were just—"

"Get the fuck away from her," Kai shouts at Timothy before he can rattle off some excuse for why he did what he did to me.

Before Timothy can try to argue again, Kai's arm slips beneath the backs of my knees, the other holding me at the waist as he hoists me into the air.

"I've got you," he promises, again and again, as he carries me back into the cabin. I'm too weak to protest his touch, but once I'm hoisted into the air I don't mind much at all. So long as he gets me far away from here—from *him*.

I'm able to think more clearly once we're safely back inside the cabin, the adrenaline and fear beginning to simmer back down. The comfort I always took in Kai's voice returns, despite the fear Timothy awakened in me. "I've got you," Kai repeats, like a mantra or a prayer. Soft and kind and full of promise.

Tears still blur my vision even after he sets me down. He gives me space to let it all out, sitting across from me until the sobs simmer down to whimpers. He gets me a glass of water and a tissue but doesn't say anything. Through the dark I struggle to make out the details of where we are. A bathroom, I slowly figure out. Me on the edge of the counter and him propped on the edge of the closed toilet seat lid.

While I down my water—hiccupping between sips—he takes my phone and sets it on the back of the toilet seat, the flashlight bathing us in light.

"Can I look at your foot?" he asks so tenderly it breaks my

heart. The fear comes back full force like a ten-ton weight when he reaches for my foot. As much as I wanted to believe I was fine, the mere thought of touch makes me want to run away.

I don't want Timothy to have that kind of power over me, though, so I nod my consent to Kai. He's incredibly careful as I extend my leg out toward him, stalling when I wince at even at the lightest brush of his skin against mine. He takes his time, waiting until the tension eases from my shoulders before he approaches again. Blood drips onto the plush white bathmat, but Kai doesn't seem to care as he gingerly cups my calf and tilts my foot toward him. I wince again when he gently pushes it back to get a better look at the slice in my heel, hissing and tugging slightly out of his grip.

"Sorry, sorry, sorry," he says quickly, but not panicked. He doesn't reach out for me again right away, instead letting me set the terms. Once again, he waits for my rushed breathing to slow before he extends his hands back out toward me, and I set my leg back into his hold. "It's deeper than I thought," he murmurs, brow furrowing as he examines the wound more closely. "And looks like there's still a piece left in here."

The thought makes me dizzy, even though I shouldn't be surprised. The way pain shoots through me at even the slightest movements should've made that obvious.

"I'm gonna grab some stuff to get this cleaned up. Okay?"

He waits until I give him another nod before standing up, carefully setting my foot back down to dangle over the edge of the counter. He moves quickly, taking my phone and the light that came with it, but stalls in the doorway. Just like Timothy did. My traitorous heart pounds when he turns around, anxious about what his next move could be. But he just frowns.

"You're gonna be okay," he whispers, eyes focused on mine.

And even when he walks away, leaving me in the dark, I know he means it.

I brace myself for Timothy to come back—to storm through the open doorway and finish what he started. But no footsteps approach. I can hear the comforting sound of Kai pulling the sliding door shut, locking it behind him followed by the rustle of him opening drawers and cabinets in the kitchen like Kiki had earlier. He's back faster than I anticipated, rushing into the room so quickly he almost loses his balance on the blood-slick tile. He sets the lit up phone on the edge of the counter beside me, and I suddenly remember that he'd given Kiki's phone to Timothy to use for light. A much needed resource wasted on a creep who used it just to corner me.

"I thought I'd finally figured out how the hell the wiring for the cabin worked," Kai begins explaining without any prompting, talking a mile a minute as he lays out the supplies he grabbed from the kitchen. "The whole thing was a mess of wires that all looked the same, and I didn't want to leave and forget which one was which, so I had Timothy run inside to grab the tweezers, but then I heard you scream and I . . ."

He exhales sharply, cutting himself off mid-explanation. A piece of me softens. He didn't ignore me. He heard me. He came after me. Just a moment too late.

"I should've just dropped everything and ran over as soon as I heard you. I'm so, so sorry I didn't."

Even in the dim light from my phone flashlight I can see tears glimmering in his eyes, hear guilt dripping from every syllable he speaks. He doesn't touch me, doesn't move in any closer. Just kneels down in front of me and looks up with eyes that beg for the forgiveness he can't ask for out loud. It breaks my heart, looking at how hurt he is. But it hurts me just as much, too—how badly I wish he could've arrived a few seconds earlier.

I'm not sure what to say—what could possibly sum up all the conflicting feelings swirling in my head and my heart? How I'm not sure who I can trust here after that voicemail from Mikey and what Timothy's done. How it feels impossible to not believe that Kai is exactly who I want him to be when he looks at me with those kind brown eyes and touches me with the kind of tenderness I've always wished for.

So, I don't say anything. Instead, I let my body speak for me. I reach down to where his hand is resting beside mine on the counter, squeezing just enough to say what my body can't: that I'm okay. And that I hope we'll be okay too.

The simple touch is enough for Kai. He gives me a thin smile, eyes still watery as he wipes them before getting back to the much more urgent (and unpleasant) task at hand.

"This'll probably sting a bit," he warns as he settles himself back down on the ground, carefully lifting my leg up to get a better look at my heel. "Bite down on a towel, scream, hold onto my hand—whatever you need," he reassures, and I nod around a gulp.

Kai's hands move in a blur, too quickly for me to make out what he's doing in the dimly lit room. I can hear the snap of a package pulling open, and something coming unrolled, but before I can put together what it all means pain jolts through me. White hot enough to make me arch away from the wall I was leaning against and let out a choked, pained whimper.

"I'm sorry, almost done," Kai promises, sounding just as panicked as I am. I can feel his fingers trembling against my leg as he struggles to move efficiently and painlessly. The edge of what must be tweezers dig into my skin as they root through the gash for the stray piece of glass.

Sweat breaks out along my brow, my chest heaving as I struggle to keep my breathing as controlled as possible—to focus on the steady in-out-in-out instead of the pain rippling through my leg. Finally, I hear a soft *clunk*. The sound of the blood-stained glass hitting the tile floor. I sag against the counter, leg dropping like dead weight as Kai lets go of me to scoop up the glass.

Once the glass is stashed safely in a paper towel, Kai cleans off the wound with a warm towel and wraps it with an adhesive bandage. Despite his shaking hands, his touch is still gentler than anyone else who's cared for me before. He reads the slight pulses in my nerves—the unexpected jolts of pain—and slows or softens his movements in response. I wonder if he plans to go into medicine, to handle patients with the same care. To whisper softly that they'll be all right. Or is this something reserved just for me?

It's a pretty thought, but I don't—*can't*—let it linger. Not after tonight. Not when the world proved that a popular boy's attention isn't the miracle I once thought it was. Not with Mikey's warning voicemail echoing in my head.

My attention fixes on the paper towel Kai sets down on the counter beside me. In just a few seconds it's almost soaked through with blood, the shard much bigger than I anticipated. Just looking at the jagged edges makes bile crawl up my throat. I'm not sure what hurts worse—the phantom pain of the glass, or the phantom sensation of Timothy's lips against mine.

"You don't have to tell me anything you're not comfortable with," Kai says, breaking the silence, after wiping down his own sweat-drenched face with a towel. He reaches into a basket beside the toilet and hands me a fresh towel of my own, waiting until I've wiped down my brow and damp collarbone to continue. "But . . ." He trails off, glancing down between my foot and the small drops of blood staining the tile. Keeping his gaze on the floor when he finally finds the courage to speak again. "What did he do?"

I swallow hard and dig my fingers into my arms to keep myself grounded. To stop the nausea from overwhelming me again. I don't want to linger on it—to relive that moment and the sourness of his breath—but I know if I can tell anyone it's Kai. Mami would find a way to twist the story and make me the villain—tell me that I led Timothy on or did something to make him think this was what I wanted. Mikey would do the same thing he does to anyone who pisses him off—solve the problem with his fists. I have no one else.

So, I tell Kai everything. About how I'd seen that the sliding door was open and assumed the worst. How I came prepared with a weapon, in case I had to defend myself. Timothy startling me—the scream he'd heard all the way from the shed. How Timothy had me trapped in a mess of shattered glass, unable to run. That he kissed me, hard and messy. That I did my best to push against him but all he did was hold me tighter. That I wasn't sure what else he would've done if Kai hadn't come back when he did. How sick it made me feel. How I can still feel his touch lingering all over me.

When I finish, Kai doesn't say anything. He turned his gaze up toward me when I mentioned the scream he must've heard, guilt written all over him, but his eyes wander when I get to the kiss. His shoulders tremble as I continue, to the point that he's practically vibrating by the time I finish. He mutters something under his breath that sounds a lot like "I'm going to kill him" before rocketing up at breakneck speed. Before I can ask him where he's going—or ask him to stay—he's rushing out of the bathroom and storming toward the deck.

"Kai!" I call out to him as I hop off the counter and do my best to trail after him. I can only go so fast without putting any weight on my foot, and he has an athlete's stamina and rage powering him.

"Timothy!" Kai shouts as he throws the sliding door open so hard I worry the glass will shatter. The frame wobbles as the door snaps back, suddenly loose on its track from the force of being yanked open, but the glass thankfully stays in one piece.

I grab onto anything I can find—table edges and chair arms—for balance and guidance as the light from my phone fades once he gets outside. By the time I make it over to the sliding door, Kai looks like he's a ticking time bomb seconds from exploding. There's a red-hot flush to his skin as he paces the edge of the deck and points the flashlight at something over the edge.

"Where is he?" I ask, lingering in the doorway and gripping the wall for balance.

Kai leans over the railing, his grip on the wood banister so tight it looks like he could snap it. With a scoff, he leans back up and points the light toward the ground so I can see what he sees. A set of fresh footprints in the mud, headed into the woods.

"Gone."

EXHIBIT H: AUTOPSY REPORT

DECEASED: Timothy Leonard Gibson

AGE: 17

SEX: M

DATE AND HOUR OF DEATH: October 31, approx. 10:00 p.m.

DATE AND HOUR OF AUTOPSY: November 1, 4:31 p.m.

FINDINGS:

Victim was discovered approx. 100 feet from the cabin where he was staying with friends for the weekend. Discovery was made by first responding officer, Frank Doughty, after witnesses claimed he had gone missing over the course of the night. Defensive wounds on the palms, wrists, and arms indicate a struggle. Multiple injuries to the skull, head, and neck are consistent with a heavyweight weapon such as an axe or hatchet.

MANNER OF DEATH: Homicide

CAUSE OF DEATH: Blunt force trauma

17

Strangely, not knowing where Timothy is sets me more on edge than him lurking somewhere inside. As Kai and I follow the trail of footprints to the opposite end of the cabin—toward where Timothy and Kai had been working on getting the lights turned back on—I keep scanning the edge of the woods. Searching for shapes in the dark with sharp teeth and wandering hands. A few times I swear I see something shift, running between the trees for cover, but Kai doesn't so much as flinch as he stomps back toward the side of the cabin.

The dark is making me see things.

I regret following after Kai as I struggle to avoid putting my bandaged foot down on the paved path. Small pebbles and twigs pierce the tender skin of my uninjured foot. It's hard enough to stay on the path with barely any light to guide me, let alone on one foot. Still, I try to stay as close to Kai as I possibly can—a tougher task than I anticipated thanks to the extra four or so inches he has on me.

"Timothy?" Kai shouts again as we turn a corner. He flashes the light from my phone all across the edge of the cabin and along the driveway where we first arrived.

The footsteps we'd been following end abruptly, becoming farther and farther apart before disappearing altogether into the trees. As if Timothy started leaping like a frog, only to jump straight into the woods. It wouldn't be a smart move to go wandering into those woods even in broad daylight.

Then again, Timothy Gibson is anything but smart.

"Son of a bitch," Kai mutters to himself.

He stops in front of a metal box attached to the exterior wall of the cabin. The fuse box, if I had to guess. There's a small collection of tools gathered at the base of the box—some duct tape, a hammer, and a bolt cutter—along with several sets of prints in the mud below it.

"What's wrong?" I ask.

"Timothy fucked everything up," Kai mutters, pulling the box open fully so I can see the damage.

All the wires have been pulled free, as if someone reached in, grabbed whatever they could, and yanked.

If there's any way to salvage the wires, it won't be easy and it won't be quick. Several have been snapped entirely, their remains dangling off the edge of the box or scattered in the mud. I don't know much about electrical wiring but it doesn't take an engineering degree to see we're screwed.

Kai groans, slamming the lid of the metal box closed so roughly it bounces back open, squeaking eerily on rusted hinges. "Now we're stuck without power," he mutters bitterly, looking down at my phone. "With twenty percent battery left and no way to charge it." He sighs before handing the phone back to me. "Sorry."

I swallow hard at the thought of spending the rest of the night in the dark. With how remote the cabin is, surrounded by trees on all sides, there's no guarantee that there'll be decent natural light even if the clouds clear up tonight. There's always morning, but without any power our phones probably won't make it until then.

The thought of my phone dying makes me jolt, suddenly remembering why I was looking for Kai in the first place. Mikey's voicemail makes this whole thing seem even more suspicious. Could this be a part of what "they" have planned?

"My brother left me a weird voicemail earlier," I say in a whisper. Kai's the only person I trust here, but even so, I'm not spilling the entire truth.

Kai's brow furrows as he pries his attention away from the fuse box to look at me. "Everything okay?"

I bite my tongue and weigh out how to respond. What if Mikey was trying to warn me about Timothy? That he was the type to act without permission—that maybe I'd been a target of his all along. How Mikey would've managed to learn that in a matter of minutes since I left is a total mystery, but how he was able to figure out anything from so far away is just as confusing. Either way, that doesn't change the suspicion still lingering in the pit of my stomach.

"I think so," I finally reply, my response just the right amount of vague that Kai doesn't question me. "Is there somewhere we can go to find service? So I can call him back?"

He sighs and runs a hand along his neck. "Mom'll kill me if we leave the cabin like this." He pauses, looking intently at the wires like it's a puzzle he can solve with telekinesis like a character from one of his comics, before finally giving in with a groan. "But we should probably head home anyway."

I breathe a quiet sigh of relief. Sneaking back into the house without Mami noticing will be a pain, but at least I can let down my guard sooner rather than later. My muscles relax as Kai closes up the fuse box and starts heading back toward the cabin. Yet instead of following him, I find myself lingering in place. Staring at the snapped wires sticking out of the edge of the metal box.

"Why would Timothy do this?" I ask, the torn wires still not making any sense to me.

Timothy clearly isn't the smartest, and he has no issues violating other people's space, but what does he gain from leaving all of us—himself included—in the dark? Does he think it's payback for me rejecting him and Kai calling him out? He's not a good person, that I know without a doubt. But is he really so reckless that he'd destroy the one thing that would've helped us all out?

"Because he's a dickhead who thinks fucking with people is funny," Kai scoffs without a moment of hesitation, his brow still knotted with what's either stress or anger, or, most likely, both.

Biting my lip, I look back toward where the footprints disappeared into the woods. "You really think it was him?"

His annoyance softens, his shoulders dropping slightly as he stops massaging his temples to look over at me. "Who else could it be?"

I shrug to buy myself some time, but my eyes stray to the tree line. Something in my gut tells me to hold there, that there's something, or someone, lingering just past what I can see. But there's no distant snapping of twigs or feet clomping through the damp leaves. No matter how hard I crane my neck and squint my eyes, we're alone.

"You're right," I say a beat too late. Kai seems puzzled when

I rush to join him but decides not to question it. He jogs toward me and offers up his arm to help me hobble back to the cabin. But even after we get back inside and lock the sliding door behind us, I can't shake the feeling that something was watching us from the dark.

EXHIBIT I: FOOTPRINT ANALYSIS

MILLCREEK PD: CASE A06729

Examination into footprints found along the exterior edge of the cabin located at 178 North Albee Way confirm that they are a match for the footprints found beside the body of TIMOTHY GIBSON. Measurements and tread patterns are consistent with New Balance women's size seven sneakers.

Based on further analysis of the sole patterns, we can confirm these prints are consistent with the sneakers recovered from the scene, believed to belong to defendant DINA SOTO.

18

There's no sign of Timothy anywhere in the cabin. Kai insists on tracking him down before we head out.

"No way I'm leaving that asshole here to keep wrecking the place," he says with a huff.

Kai throws open every door and looks around every corner for him, the rage beneath his skin pulsing louder and louder with every empty room he passes. "Stop bullshitting me, Timothy, I know you're here," Kai shouts into the empty living room before storming up the stairs to the second floor.

Kiki and Carla are hovering in the doorway to their room by the time Kai makes it upstairs. I pause on the landing, slowing my pace at the sight of them.

"Why're you yelling?" Kiki asks in annoyance. Once I finally manage to catch up to them, I can't help but notice the fresh red mark on the curve of Carla's neck.

What's the point of threatening me to not spill their secret when they're not even bothering to hide their tracks?

If Kai notices anything off about his sister and her best friend, he doesn't comment. I wonder briefly if he *does* know—if what everyone says about twins is true and they have some kind of secret-revealing psychic bond. But I know better than to ask him outright.

"Have you seen your boyfriend?" Kai asks Carla, fingers clenched into fists.

Carla shrugs, crossing her arms. "No. Why?"

"He . . ." Kai stops suddenly, all the rage draining out of him as he whips around to face me. The back of my neck prickles from the intensity of his gaze as he tilts his head slightly to the side once he meets my eyes. A silent question, I realize. Asking if it's all right to tell them what happened.

The thought of telling Carla and Kiki about what Timothy did makes me almost as nervous as the thought of facing him again. The possibility that they might shut me down—tell me that I misinterpreted what Timothy said or did—because boys like Timothy would never look at girls like me, especially when they have girlfriends like Carla. We all think it—they're just cruel enough to say it.

I shake my head subtly enough to not catch the girls' attention. Kai sighs, his shoulders deflating as he turns back to them just as Kiki narrows her eyes in my direction. "He tore out a bunch of the wiring on the breaker. So, we're fucked."

Kiki whips her attention back to her brother so fast her braids hit Carla's cheek. "He did *what*?!"

Carla isn't even fazed by the slap from Kiki's hair, shaking her head like a dismayed mother looking down on her toddler. She lets out a groan before pinching the bridge of her nose. "That asshole."

In the blink of an eye, Kiki starts to spiral. She runs her hands down the side of her face, bringing them back up to massage her temples for a few seconds before ultimately digging her fingers into her scalp and pacing across the hallway. "Jesus, Kai, Mom and Dad are gonna murder us."

"I know," Kai says with an eyeroll before picking up where

he left off and scanning the bathroom opposite their room for any sign of Timothy. "That's why I'm looking for the guy who did it so I can serve him up to them on a silver platter. Because I'm *not* taking the fall for this." He slams the door to the bathroom shut when he doesn't find any sign of Timothy, and quickly moves on to the next room.

"He probably went for a walk to smoke," Carla explains, still shaking her head in frustration. "That's usually what he does when he's upset."

"In the middle of the woods? At night?" Kiki asks with a raised brow.

Carla shrugs. "White guys love that shit."

She has a point there. Still, going out alone in the woods doesn't seem like something even the most reckless idiot would do. Unless he's trying to hide from us, now that we know what he did. As much as I can't stand him, I can't blame him for not wanting to face an angry Kiki Thompson.

Kai sighs and collapses onto the nearby wall, running a hand down his face. "Well as soon as he shows up, we're getting out of here," Kai orders. Kiki and Carla don't respond to him but share a skeptical look. "Do you want to stay here alone in the dark?" Kai snaps when he notices their expressions.

"Fine," Kiki replies bitterly, crossing her arms and heading back toward the kitchen. "But you're driving."

"My pleasure." Kai's voice is dripping with sarcasm, but neither Kiki nor Carla snap back.

The girls keep themselves busy by heading into the kitchen, packing up the snacks and cups littering the counter. Outside, I can hear the first warning signs of a storm. Rumbles of thunder and the quiet patter of raindrops on the window. Unless he wants to get soaked while stoned and lost, Timothy will be back sooner rather than later. Kai gestures with his chin toward the couch before holding his arm out to help guide me to it, but I shake my head.

"I'm gonna go get changed." I point over my shoulder toward the staircase. I've had enough running around in just a towel and a bathing suit for one night.

Kai nods, rubbing the back of his neck sheepishly. "There should be some candles in the attic. I can bring you some, if you need them."

I nod and give him a smile. Can't hurt to give my phone a break, especially when I still need to call Mikey once we have service again. As I turn around, Kai opens his mouth slightly, looking as though he's going to say something else. But Kai's mouth closes as quickly as it parted. Instead, he gives me a tight smile of his own before heading toward the staircase, most likely to head up to the attic. A bolt of lightning rips through the sky as he turns to leave, bathing the living room in bright white light. My shadow stretches long across the hallway—long enough to reach Kai. My darkness consuming him whole.

19

Kai comes back with more than just candles. A large rose gold candle is tucked beneath his arm along with an extra pillow, and a towel. Pinned between his chin and shoulder is a packet of Oreos, while his left hand struggles to daintily carry a mug of something steaming hot. My brow furrows—how did he manage to make something hot in the middle of a power outage?

"The joys of having a gas stove," Kai says when he notices my look of confusion.

"I didn't know this place came with room service," I can't help but tease as he struggles to set down the towel and pillows on the edge of my bed without spilling whatever's in the mug.

"Only the best service at the powerless Chateau de Thompson," he replies, nose wrinkled in concentration as he finally sets the mug down safely on my nightstand and breathes a sigh of relief.

I pull my knees up toward my chest, giving him room to set down his bounty before sitting down on the edge of my bed. Changing into clothes I'm used to—a baggy flannel and jeans—did wonders for setting me at ease.

I tried to call Mikey back a handful of times, but the No

Service still displayed prominently in the corner of my screen held true. Instead, I've tried to reason with the panicked side of me. Mikey could've been wrong, or lying to get me to turn around and come home, or even a combination of the two. Or, more likely, he knew about Timothy all along and the worst of that experience—as bad as it was—is over now.

Even if that was it, I hope Mikey isn't too panicked that I haven't called him back. Hopefully he remembers from the few times we've visited the river that the service is awful up here. Still, I can't shake the guilt burning inside me. I've had my fair share of nights spent alone in the house, knowing something awful was happening and there was nothing I could do about it. How terrible it felt to be so powerless. How badly I wanted to sneak out through my window and take matters into my own hands.

Like me, Mikey doesn't have a license, so the chances of him doing what I couldn't and coming to find me are slim. But then again, whether something is legal or not hasn't stopped him before.

I quickly shake off that line of thought. Once Timothy's back, we'll be out of here and I'll be home before Mikey can do anything stupid.

While I'd been avoiding him earlier, I'm looking forward to Timothy showing up. At least once he's back, we'll finally be able to leave.

Even with Mikey's voicemail still hanging over me, there's something strangely comforting about being trapped inside during a storm—listening to the tree branches and wind whipping past my window while I'm bundled safe in my bed—or, as safe as I can be.

While Kai lays out the rest of his cargo, I take a closer

look at the mug he set down beside me. Steam dances above an almost full-to-bursting layer of marshmallows—several of them already melting into the warm liquid.

"Hot chocolate. My grandma's recipe," Kai explains when he catches me looking. "It's got so much sugar it can take a year off your life, but it's pretty damn worth it."

I test that theory by taking a tentative sip. Sure enough, it's as perfect as he promises. Richly sweet and smooth without being too overpowering. A dash of cinnamon and something I can't quite place for added depth, all the flavors a perfect complement to the gooey half-melted marshmallows. From what I've tasted of Mrs. Thompson's cooking at Sunny Hills, it's no surprise that she makes the best hot chocolate in town—probably in the state. And that it tastes like it has several cups' worth of sugar. Every time I've sampled her food, she's been sure to remind me that the key to becoming a good cook is to stop listening to your head and listen to your stomach.

"Use as much butter as you damn well please," she'd once said after a crowd had gathered to sample her famous baked mac and cheese.

I nod in agreement before I've even swallowed. "Definitely worth it."

As he sits down beside me, I can tell Kai is trying to bite back a laugh, his attempt at hiding his smile failing adorably. I quirk my brow, silently asking him what he's laughing about, and he points to the corner of his own mouth. Sure enough, when I match his movement there's a glob of marshmallow clinging to the edge of my lip. My cheeks are almost as warm as the mug as I quickly wipe my mouth with the back of my hand.

Kai pulls the thick candle out of the bundle of pillows and sets it down on the nightstand. He does the honors of lighting it, pulling a matchbox from his pocket and swiping a match to life. The scent of vanilla settles over the room within seconds.

Once the candle is lit, Kai juts his chin toward the array of supplies spread out across my bed. "You need anything else?"

This time it's my turn to stifle a laugh. At this rate, if he brought me anything else I wouldn't have any space to actually lie down on the bed. "I think you covered everything," I reply, not bothering to hold back my smile.

Kai doesn't seem to pick up on the humor, though. Instead of meeting my smile with one of his own, he ducks his head to his chest sheepishly, averting his gaze from mine as he mumbles a "sorry."

I open my mouth, ready to assure him that he hasn't done anything wrong, but all I do is trip over myself, garbled mishmashed sounds tumbling out instead of what I originally meant to say. Kai glances up at me with a furrowed brow and I clamp my mouth shut before I can make even more of an ass out of myself. I inhale slowly, using the exhale to collect my thoughts, and set my mug carefully back down on the nightstand.

Once I'm sure I won't sound like I'm short-circuiting, I shift in closer to him, resisting the urge to reach out and touch his shoulder. "You don't have to be sorry for bringing me extra pillows," I reassure him, guilt tugging at my heart.

"I mean about everything," he says. "I said this was going to be a chill cabin weekend and it's just . . ." He trails off with a sigh before flopping against the army of pillows behind him and blowing a raspberry. "A mess."

I shrug as I settle down beside him. I make sure to keep a

careful amount of distance between us, propping myself up on my elbow so I can look down at him. "That's not your fault."

While I'm still on edge from everything that happened with Timothy, not to mention my run-in with Kiki and Carla in their room and Mikey's voicemail, Kai's kindness has never wavered. He's the one bit of proof I have that Mikey could be wrong. You can't fake the kind of sincerity Kai has. Even if you're a fantastic actor. From the moment he picked me up, Kai's tried to make me feel welcome. Safe. It's not his fault that the others seem determined to do the opposite.

Out in the hallway, Carla and Kiki's voices trail over from the staircase. I can just make out Carla telling Kiki about the conditioning treatment she wasted her money on last month when the door behind them closes, sealing off their conversation. Kai leans up at the sound of their voices, just to flop back down, rolling his eyes with a sigh. "I love my sister, but her friends are assholes."

The harshness catches me off guard. While I could tell he wasn't as close to Timothy and Carla, I'd assumed they were all friends to some degree. Especially considering that they're all a part of the same elite lunch table—Kiki and Carla holding court as they're flanked by the wealthiest and most popular students Millcreek has to offer.

"Aren't they your friends too?" I ask with a furrowed brow.

"No," he says quickly, shuddering as if the thought is chilling. "Definitely not." His nose wrinkles for a moment before he loses himself in his thoughts. He looks up at the ceiling, folding his arms tightly across his chest as he whispers, "I . . . don't really have a lot of friends."

"That's impossible," I reply instantly. Saying Kai Thompson doesn't have friends is like saying that I have hundreds: factually untrue. Kai can barely make it to class on time with how many people stop him to say hi or catch up with him about sports or his plans for the weekend.

Yet Kai seems genuinely perplexed by my perspective. He turns to me, his lips curling slightly with a hint of amusement. "How so?"

"You're so . . ." I don't know how to finish that sentence. Explaining Kai's social status is like explaining why we breathe air. Why the sky is blue. It just is. "You're popular."

Kai shakes his head bashfully, laughing quietly to himself. "I'm not popular."

"Uh, hello, you were homecoming king." *Without* campaigning, I neglect to add. It was as if everyone was following an unspoken social code. Kai Thompson was the kind, charming new transfer student. It didn't matter that someone like Timothy was probably the more obvious and clichéd choice—Kai just made sense. And, for once, the whole school agreed.

Kai shrugs sheepishly, a rosy tint blooming along his cheeks as he rubs at the side of his neck—a go-to move when he's nervous, I'm realizing. "Yeah, but that's just because people were being nice."

"People are never just nice at Millcreek."

I say it without thinking. Without realizing how much bite my words have. It's a subconscious response—like picking at a scab. The students at Millcreek High have never been kind. To me, to Joel, to anyone. If they were, they wouldn't have just looked at me with pity after we lost Joel—they'd have tried to make amends. If they were, they wouldn't still be judging *me* for what Papi did. Our classmates are lots of things, but I can say without a shadow of a doubt that they've never been nice just for the sake of it. Cruelty is their default.

Kai detects the unease in my tone, looking as though he's going to say something, before thinking over a new response.

"I guess I'm not that close with anyone," he says in a whisper so quiet, it's as if this is some kind of private confession.

I move closer to him until I'm leaning on the pillow opposite his. "What about all those guys you have lunch with?"

"Mostly Kiki's friends." He shrugs. "Some of them are okay, but . . . I don't know. I always feel like I'm putting on some kind of front for them. The whole 'super fratty jock' thing."

"You mean you're *not* a super fratty jock?" I tease, nudging my elbow against his.

Kai turns back to me with a knowing look, his face suddenly so close to mine it sets my heart on fire. "Did you *see* my Miles Morales costume?" he jokes.

Just thinking about the skintight fabric he'd been wearing earlier this afternoon makes the heat return to my cheeks. His current ensemble isn't any better in terms of not drawing my attention—still dressed in his damp swimming trunks with a half-unbuttoned flannel layered over it now—but something about the costume manages to make my stomach flutter just from the thought.

"There just aren't that many people I feel like I can be myself with," Kai continues when I don't say anything. He turns back to me with a shy smile—nudging me this time with his shoulder. Except, he doesn't pull away like I did, letting his arm stay pressed up against mine. Our fingers are so close it would only take a subtle twitch for mine to be wrapped up in his. "Except you."

My heart pounds louder than my racing thoughts, louder than the rain and thunder rumbling outside. So loud I'm sure he must hear it. "Really?" I ask, wishing I didn't sound as breathless as I feel.

"You let me talk your ear off about my drawings."

"Because they're really good."

"They're—"

"Don't be modest," I interject, gently tapping my hand against his. Pushing to see how far we're willing to let each other go. "I can barely handle stick figures."

"Well, thank you." Kai rolls over onto his side properly, facing me head on. "For the compliment and for not calling me a nerd."

Before I can overthink it, I fold my arm down beneath my head like a pillow and roll over onto it. We're side by side, face to face. "I never said you weren't a nerd."

His laugh is drowned out by a clap of thunder, but I can still feel it vibrating through me—that joyous laugh that first drew me to him. His eyes flicker down for a moment, and I don't let myself think that he might've been looking at my lips. The rosiness in his cheeks has bloomed all the way down to his collarbone when he looks back up at me, and I wonder if he feels just as warm as I do.

"I just . . . I like talking to you. It feels like you like me for *me*." He cuts himself off, eyes going as wide as the full moon outside. "Not that you like me like *that*, I just meant . . ." He sighs, too embarrassed to finish that thought, and closes his eyes.

"I do like you," I whisper before I can overthink it. Because it's true. I like him. More than I've ever liked anyone else. More than I ever thought was possible. And as much as it absolutely terrifies me and goes against everything I've been told to believe, I lean into it. I want more of this—more time with him—because he's the safe space I've been looking for since I lost Joel. My one chance to understand who I am outside the suffocatingly small box I've been stuck in for years. Because Kai's the only person who sees the real me—not Joel's sister, not Papi's daughter, *me*. Someone I'm still trying to get to know myself.

Kai seems stunned, his eyes still wide. I would've thought he was frozen if he didn't blink in sudden rapid succession, looking as though he's trying to convince himself that this moment is real—a feeling I can definitely relate to.

Suddenly, my senses heighten, everything hitting me like a tidal wave. The scent of vanilla and damp wood and lilac dryer sheets. The weight of my heart pounding against my chest, begging to be set free. The heat radiating off Kai's body as he leans in closer—the warmth of his breath against my lips. Time slows to a crawl until every single one of my nerves is on fire waiting for him to reach me, only for me to throw caution to the wind and do it myself. Cupping his cheek, leaning forward, and finally, *finally*, closing the distance between us.

It's everything I imagined it could be. Everything I thought a first kiss *should* be. Soft and tender as Kai cradles my cheek like I'm something worth protecting. Sweet from the hot chocolate still lingering on my lips. Warm, in every single way.

Unlike Timothy, Kai doesn't take and take and take. He leans back slightly, as if he's ready to break the kiss, but I'm the one who pulls him back. Who doesn't want to let go yet. He doesn't touch me until I touch him, running my palm down along the side of his arm because I'm not sure what else to do with my hands. I fight the urge to pull him as close to me as possible—to feel the full weight of him against me. To erase the memory of Timothy's touch, and the way his body felt pressed to mine.

But Kai deserves better than that. Kissing him is something that deserves to be savored—a moment I'll remember forever. Not just a palate cleanser to erase something I want to forget.

The longer we kiss, the more the world falls away. The claps of thunder don't make me jump. We don't notice the ramped-up patter of rain hitting the roof, or the wind howling through the trees. The lingering scent of vanilla fades in favor of the chlorine clinging to our skin, and the subtle tang of cologne still on Kai's collar. All I can focus on is the brush of his skin and his mouth against mine—how perfectly we slot together. How badly I've wanted this, and how it's more perfect than I ever dreamed it could be.

We're so wrapped up in one another—testing the limits and tasting each other—that neither of us hears the creak of approaching footsteps. Or the whispered voices. Not until someone clears their throat loud enough to get our attention. We fly apart at breakneck speed, Kai smacking against the headboard with a thud and yelp of pain that would have me racing to him if I wasn't so worried about getting *away* from him. I rocket off the bed, unscathed, and glance over at him once I'm on my shaky feet. He's groaning quietly, rubbing at a spot on his head, but thankfully it doesn't look like anything more serious than a bump.

I didn't think it was possible for my heart to beat any faster, until I look up and see Kiki and Carla leaning against the doorway to my room. It feels like it's stopped beating entirely—the whiplash of going from bliss to fear knocking me so off balance the edges of the room begin to spin. I pull the edge of my shirt over my exposed shoulder and do my best to flatten my mussed hair. There's nothing I can do for my swollen lips and flaming cheeks, though.

"Having fun?" Carla teases with a knowing smirk.

Kiki, meanwhile, doesn't look nearly as amused. Her expression is impossible to read as she focuses her attention on her brother as he sits up and pulls his open flannel closed across his chest.

"Ever heard of knocking?" he snaps, glaring at Kiki as he crosses the room and shifts to position himself in front of me, blocking me from their gaze. His hand rests lightly against my arm—a subtle touch of solidarity. I rest my hand over his, letting his touch keep me grounded.

"If you wanted privacy, you should've closed the door," Kiki replies, rolling her eyes.

From what I can tell, she doesn't seem upset. Bored, maybe. Unsurprised, most likely. Either way, it's a small relief to see that she isn't throwing a fit about walking in on us. I've pissed her off enough as it is for one night.

"We're doing facials in our room," Carla announces, pivoting to a new subject with an unusual amount of excitement. "My mom brought back a ton of beauty products from her last business trip to Korea," she explains with a grin.

"Want to join?" Kiki asks, leaning over to look past Kai and directly at me. Her tone isn't exactly inviting, but it isn't malicious either. Still, the suddenness of it catches me by surprise.

"Uh . . ."

Kai seems just as puzzled as I am by the invitation. He looks at me with a mix of confusion and suspicion, as if to silently ask, *What is my sister up to?*

But he doesn't know what I saw. How panicked Kiki and Carla were when they realized they'd been found out. They'd seemed ready to kill me to keep me quiet just half an hour ago, but maybe now they're changing tactics—buying my silence with kindness. Either way, it's not like I have much of a choice. We're not going anywhere until Timothy gets back, and I've already started off on the worst foot possible with Kiki. Assuming my paranoia is just getting the best of me and this actually *is* some kind of olive branch, turning down their offer kills any possibility of mending the broken bridge between us. And now that I know Kai feels the same way I do, now that I've had a taste of what we could be, I need to make nice with Kiki.

"Y-yeah. That sounds fun," I say with my best attempt at a smile.

Kai's eyes widen, looking as though he's going to ask if I'm sure. I give his hand a gentle squeeze—a silent confirmation that I know what I'm doing—before following them into the hall. Kiki and Carla lead the way back to their room, but I linger in the doorway to look back at where Kai is perched on the edge of my bed.

"I'll be fine," I mouth to him before following the girls back to their room. Maybe if I make it a promise, I can make sure it's true.

EXHIBIT J: BLOOD ANALYSIS REPORT

The defendant Dina Soto was found covered in blood at the scene on the evening of October 31. Several blood samples were collected from the defendant's clothes, skin, and hair. A total of four sources were identified.

In order of volume found on the defendant, the donors were as follows:

Specimen A: Inconclusive. Further testing needed.
Specimen B: Carla Gutierrez
Specimen C: Kiki Thompson
Specimen D: Kai Thompson

20

Kiki and Carla have made the most out of their shared room in the short time we've been here. Sequined mini dresses with matching heels in the closet and stacks of glittery eyeshadow palettes worth nearly three figures beside a pouch full of concealers, foundations, and moisturizers that must be worth twice that. It's a glimpse into the type of girlhood I never had.

"Sorry for the mess," Kiki says casually as she scoops up a pile of jeans and crop tops beside the entryway and tosses them onto the lavender comforter.

"Drink?" Carla offers as she pours one for herself from the makeshift bar they've set up on top of the dresser. Dozens of bottles of liquors, sodas, and juices are lined up between crumpled receipts and half-melted candles bathing the room in a soft orange glow.

The normalcy of it all makes the back of my neck prickle. They're acting as if Kiki didn't threaten me less than an hour ago. Like we're not stuck in this cabin in the dark in the middle of the storm. Like we're not strangers.

"Sure," I say before I can regret it. Going along with whatever they want is the safer bet, and maybe a few careful sips will at least make playing along come more naturally.

"Pick your poison." Carla gestures to the array of options.

My stomach tightens, and I quickly cross my arms across my middle. "Not tequila."

Carla nods before picking up a clear bottle from the end of the lineup. "Gin it is."

While Kiki finishes tidying up the room and Carla works on my drink, the storm rages on. Flashes of lightning make us all jump, followed by rumbles of thunder that seem three times as loud as they had been earlier in the night. The rain is coming down hard enough to even drown out the steady *badum* of my heart echoing in my ears.

"That asshole better be back soon," Carla mutters as she pulls aside the lace curtain covering the window beside the bed.

"Timothy's still not back?" I ask.

I'd assumed Timothy would've shown up while Kai and I were in my room. It would've been difficult to find his way to the cabin before the storm started, but now getting back would be nearly impossible. Between the wind and the mud covering his tracks, if he's not lost by now, he will be if he doesn't get back ASAP. As much as I don't want to be locked in the same space with him, I'd never wish for someone to be stranded in the woods in this kind of storm.

Not to mention that him getting back means me getting out of here. And with Kiki subtly pushing the door to the room closed, I hear Mikey's voice echoing in my ears again. *You're not safe there.*

"Not yet," Carla says without looking away from the window. From the way she chews on her glossy lower lip and her fingers tap a rapid beat against her arm, I can tell she's as uneasy as I am.

"Should we go looking for him?" I suggest, unsure why we haven't already.

“In the pouring rain? No thank you,” Kiki says as casually as if we were talking about going out to find a lost lip gloss instead of a person. She softens when she catches sight of Carla, though. “He’s probably hiding out somewhere until the storm passes.”

“Right . . .” But Carla doesn’t seem convinced, still gazing out the window.

Kiki wraps an arm around Carla’s shoulders, squeezing her to her side. “He’ll be fine,” she whispers as she gently pulls Carla away from the window.

Carla’s gaze lingers on the woods until Kiki sits her down on the edge of the bed and hands her the drink she’d been making me. While Carla chugs her half-finished concoction, Kiki does the honors of pouring me a new drink, handing it over with a smirk.

“Face mask or lip mask?” Kiki asks as I take my first sip.

The abrupt change in topic nearly makes me choke on my drink. “W-what?” I croak out between coughs, the alcohol stinging its way down my already-dry throat.

“What do you want to start with?” Kiki holds up a variety of pastel-colored packages, each of them with an over-the-top illustration. Rapunzel-like hair and lips so plump they look like sausages.

“Uh, lip mask,” I reply, my chest aching from the combined burn of another round of coughs and alcohol.

“Great choice,” she praises before guiding me toward the freshly cleared-off vanity.

She sets down the array of products in her arms, busying herself with tearing open the lip mask package. In the vanity mirror’s reflection, I watch as Carla finishes off her drink with a wince, wiping the corner of her mouth and shaking herself slightly. The chug seems to have done the trick, her eyes alight with a new kind of fire instead of the concern that kept her glued to the window. All thoughts of Timothy seem to be abandoned as she slinks toward the vanity and perches herself over my shoulder. Meanwhile, I find myself wishing to whatever deity is listening that he'll get back soon. That I get to *leave* soon.

Unlike Kai, their smiles are harder to believe. Their sincerity is laced with hints of who they really are—the cruel mean girls who rule the student body on their perfectly crafted campaign of fear.

"You have such nice lips," Carla praises, running her fingertips along her own. "Mine were basically nonexistent until I begged my mom for lip filler for my sixteenth."

I can't help but examine my own lips in the mirror, cheeks flushing as I realize they're still swollen from earlier. Pink and chapped from being occupied with Kai's for so long. I glance quickly over at Kiki as she opens up a light pink tube of clear gel and taps a bit onto her wrist before turning to me, wondering if she can tell the difference. What has changed about me.

Kiki leans toward me, a glob of the thick clear cream on her fingertip. I hold my breath as she dabs the cream across my lips, so close I can smell the tequila lingering on her breath. I follow orders when she instructs me to rub my lips together. I'd watched her pump out the cream from a standard labeled tube. If they're planning something like Mikey warned, it probably isn't this. Not unless they managed to sneak something into a fully sealed tube.

Small beads mixed into the cream scrape my dry lips, making them feel more raw than they did when we started. When I catch sight of myself in the mirror I almost laugh at the absurdity of my reflection—my lips plumped and swollen like a dead fish. Out of context, I must look like I got stung by a bee, or had a serious allergic reaction to something. If this is what they're up to—making me look like a monster just to make fun of me, or take pictures and spread it around the school, so be it. I've been through worse. And at least I'll be able to breathe a little easier knowing the worst is over. That I can still make it home unscathed.

Carla drags a beanbag from the opposite end of the room toward the vanity, collapsing onto it and spilling some of her drink down the front of the deep red tube dress she's pulled on over her swimsuit. The drink doesn't stain though, the front of her chest already wet from the outline of her bikini top.

"So, Kai really likes you," she says with a mischievous grin, arching an eyebrow at me as she takes another sip.

I resist the urge to take a sip of my own drink and risk ruining the lip mask, tapping my finger against the side of the cup instead. "We're just friends," I mumble, thankful that the lip mask makes it tough to talk clearly.

"Friends who make out with each other?" Carla teases while Kiki pointedly ignores us, her face as unreadable as stone. She doesn't even look over, too busy pulling open a packet of under-eye patches.

I bite my tongue, resisting the urge to remind Carla that she and Kiki are *also* just friends. They didn't seem to have any issue making out with each other, even though one of them has a boyfriend. A boyfriend that's currently stranded outside in the middle of a storm.

A deep clap of thunder saves me from having to reply, drowning out the quiet music playing from the wireless speaker on the dresser.

"So, spill. What's going on between you two?" Carla pries again, nudging her fist against my knee.

The lip mask suddenly feels like it's burning when Kiki returns to my side, a set of gold comma-shaped patches beneath her eyes. She grips my chin so unexpectedly I almost jolt off the edge of my seat, but Kiki's grip is firm enough to keep me in place. The patches she applies beneath my own eyes are so cold they send instant chills down my spine. Wet and slimy and making my skin crawl. I dare a glance up at her, unable to keep my gaze averted for long with her this close to me, but there's no hint in her deep brown eyes about how she feels about Carla's prying. It's almost as if she's looking right through me.

"Nothing," I finally reply once Kiki has let go of me to wipe her damp fingers off on her sweatpants. "We're just . . ." I hesitate, unsure how to describe what exactly we're doing, and how much to reveal. Based on everyone's reaction to my presence tonight, no one had any idea that Kai and I were . . . whatever it is that we are. I'm not sure how much he's told them, or whether he prefers to keep that side of his life to himself. "We're getting to know each other," I finally settle on, a vague enough answer.

"Clearly," Carla says with a snort. Suddenly, I'm grateful for the eyepatches. At least they cover up most of the color spreading across my cheeks.

Kiki still doesn't say anything as she pulls up a fluffy pink stool and sits down beside me. Coming in here, I'd been terrified of what she might say once she had me alone. But the silence is even more unnerving. We're only a few rooms down from Kai—assuming he didn't head downstairs. Even if he did, he's close enough that they wouldn't try anything . . . would they?

"Kai had a really hard time at our old school," Kiki says abruptly. I whip around to face her, but she's not looking at me. She's laser focused on mixing a mint green cream with the precision of a neurosurgeon.

"Oh, um, he never told me that," I say when Kiki doesn't continue, unsure what kind of response she's expecting.

Kai, with his infinite charm and infectious laugh and bright-as-the-sun smile, doesn't seem like the type to have a hard time with anything. Whether Kiki means he struggled with his grades—which has never seemed to be an issue for him, from what I've seen—or whether she means socially. It's impossible for me to imagine a world where Kai isn't beloved by everyone he meets. Where he's bled dry of all the warmth that draws people to him.

"He doesn't like to talk about it," Kiki continues, setting the cream down on the vanity and handing me a paper towel. She gestures for me to wipe off my mouth when I stare at the towel blankly. Quickly, I clean the lip product off and take in a quick deep inhale, grateful to have one less thing weighing on me.

"Can't blame him," Carla mutters from over my shoulder. She seems to know more about what happened at Kai and Kiki's old school than I do.

"What happened?" I ask tentatively, torn between not wanting to pry about something Kai hasn't chosen to open up about and wanting to know more.

"People were just really shitty to him after he came out," Kiki explains, her voice unusually hoarse as she tosses a fresh packet of under-eye patches to Carla.

I swallow hard. Flashes of my own past—of Joel—echo in the back of my mind. Kiki still doesn't look directly at me as she picks the cream back up and brushes a swipe of it along my chin, focused on applying an even layer across my face as she continues.

"They made his life hell. No matter what we did, no matter

how many teachers we talked to, nothing ever changed. At one point Kai was skipping school almost every other day just because he didn't want to have to deal with it. The principal was threatening to expel him if he missed any more classes, even after we told him a thousand times that he was skipping because he didn't feel safe there." She pauses with the brush pressed to my cheek, and exhales sharply. "So, our parents pulled us out and moved us across the state to be closer to our grandma. Because we knew if we stayed, things would never change. They'd only get worse."

Tears spring to my eyes and I hope Kiki doesn't notice. The story is achingly familiar. I've never told mine out loud, but I wonder if I'd be able to control my emotions the way Kiki is right now. Then again, hers is easier to tell because the story has a happy ending. Kai is okay. Not just okay but thriving.

My brother is gone.

Kiki shakes herself off slightly, picking up where she left and swiping the brush along the slope of my nose. "When we started at Millcreek, I knew things had to be different. I tried so hard to protect my brother at our old school, but it meant nothing in the end. People didn't care if I threatened them, or if I landed them in detention for what they did or said to him. They just did it again, and again, and again. But we had a fresh slate here. Nobody knew who we were—what we'd been through."

She stalls again, the brush dry of product. The cream feels ice-cold on my skin, almost cold enough to burn. Kiki doesn't dip the brush back into the pot, though. Instead, she finally looks at me head on—the intensity of her gaze pinning me in place. The heat of it warming my chilled skin. Her eyes narrow slightly, something darkening behind them as she leans in just enough for me to feel the heat of her breath against my skin.

"I knew from the minute I stepped foot in that school that I wasn't going to let anyone fuck with Kai. *Anyone*."

Slowly, the missing pieces of the puzzle that is Kiki Thompson come together. How the twin sister of a boy who is as warm as pure sunshine can be so cold. Why she's so willing to tear others down, to strike fear into people she barely knows.

It's a survival tactic.

From the moment Kiki and Kai arrived at Millcreek, they were the center of attention. Our class is made up of the same hundred or so kids we spent elementary and middle school with. New kids are rare. The sudden spotlight could've easily sunk them—landed them in the same position they were in at their last school.

I can see those first few weeks of the school year from Kiki's perspective now. Showing up in a new environment with a blank slate—a chance to make yourself whoever you want, or need, to be. If I were in her position—if I had a chance to start over with Joel—maybe I would've done the same thing. Befriended Carla Gutierrez, head cheerleader and top of the social food chain. Matched her easy cruelness. Made it clear that if anyone ever dared to fuck with her, there would be a problem.

Kiki built herself a suit of armor within weeks of arriving at Millcreek. An armor that she knew would extend to Kai. It's admirable, really. How quickly she was able to rise through the ranks and establish herself as someone worthy of the entire student body's respect. To get her brother the fresh start he deserved.

"I get it," I say, more to myself than to her.

Kiki stops swirling her brush through the cream to blink up at me with a furrowed brow.

In the mirror, I watch Carla stop filing her nails, interest piqued.

I bite my tongue, weighing whether it's worth telling them about what happened to Joel. Carla already knows pieces of the story—but maybe not the full thing. And probably not the truth. Being Jose's girlfriend, I'm sure he had his own version of events to tell her. Sanitized and watered down until he looked like the type of harmless bully you laugh about once you've been out of high school long enough.

After Papi, the lines between fact and fiction faded completely. The story of what happened between Papi and those boys has always started with Joel, but that chapter has faded away over time, replaced by a new beginning. A more sensational one—about a coach driven by rage to murder his players. Everyone chooses to forget we'd already gone through one loss before losing everything.

"My brother Joel came out as gay his freshman year," I say carefully, testing the weight of the words on my tongue. "Mostly just to our family. It wasn't a secret or anything, but my mom is strict. We had trouble making friends, and keeping them," I say with a hint of bitterness. "Joel was especially shy—most people didn't even know him, let alone that he'd come out. But my dad always thought he'd find his place at Millcreek eventually. Make friends that weren't me and my little brother."

I can see Carla and Kiki stiffen at the mention of Papi. I resist the urge to scoff or roll my eyes. He's locked up in a maximum-security prison hundreds of miles away from us. They have no reason to be afraid of him.

I continue on. "My dad was coaching the soccer team, and he thought if Joel joined he'd have an easier time making friends, but . . ." I pause, inhaling sharply. "There were these two guys on the team. They . . . they made things really hard for Joel. Cornered him in the locker room, said awful stuff about him to the rest of the team. Tried to get him removed because they said they didn't want to play on a team with a . . ." I swallow hard at the thought of all the horrible things they called him, names I can't dwell on because they still hurt like a punch to the gut. "You can fill in the blank," I mutter bitterly.

"Jose said they got probation for what they did," Carla says suddenly, earning her a glare from Kiki—either for interrupting me, or for daring to protest.

"They did," I reply, fingers clenching into a fist. "But that was all the school did. Just because they weren't on the team anymore didn't mean they stopped. It only got worse after that. They found Joel in the halls. Cafeteria. After school."

My throat tightens, knowing what comes next. Words I haven't had to say out loud because everyone already knew.

"We lost Joel two weeks after those guys got kicked off the team."

"They killed him?" Kiki asks with wide eyes, likely wondering how it was possible she'd missed that detail in the infamous Millcreek Murder case.

I shake my head bitterly, eyes stinging as I lose control and let the tears roll down my cheeks. Globs of the face mask fall away from my skin, dripping down onto my hands, but I don't bother to clean up the mess. "He killed himself." The words scratch and claw their way out of my throat, leaving me as raw and aching as the day Papi told me what happened. When I realized I'd never get to hug my brother again. Never challenge him to another race down the block or argue with him over the remote. Never watch him paint another sunset or sing along to another ballad with so much force his cheeks would turn red as apples. Never get to say goodbye.

Kiki inhales sharply. Carla flinches, her attention shifting back to her cup as she swirls her half-finished drink. But I won't let their discomfort stop me from telling the truth. She can ignore the truth about what her ex-boyfriend did, but I can't. I'll never be able to forget.

"The school didn't do anything, even then. The only punishment those guys got was a week-long suspension." My fists tremble in my lap, knuckles as pale as the cream slathered across my face. "They were back at school before we even had a chance to bury Joel. I had to see them *every day*. Walk down the same halls and sit in the same cafeteria as the two assholes who took my brother away from me. And no one cared. No one did a single fucking thing about it."

I swipe quickly at my cheek, not caring if I smudge the face mask. Sniffling and struggling to keep a full-on wave of tears at bay, I compose myself before turning to face Kiki directly, eyes locked with hers. "So, I get it. You don't want history to repeat itself. And that means staying away from people like me."

Because I'm the closest thing Millcreek has to a plague. No matter what Kai thinks of me, how much he might like me, I'm a danger to Kiki's plan. To *him*. No one wants to get too close to the girl with the murderer for a dad. And anyone who does is just as ripe for the chopping block as I am. If I were Kiki, I'd hate me too. But even if I can understand it—can feel deep in my gut why she'd want to push me as far away from Kai as possible—I can't let her think that, of all the people Kai could've found, that he'd chosen the one who was willing to hurt him.

"I promise you, I'm not the problem." I lean in as close as I dare. "I'm not who you have to worry about."

We hold each other's gazes, neither of us blinking or willing to give in for what feels like hours.

"Well, time for another drink," Carla announces, snapping Kiki and I out of our locked stare. "This place is depressing enough already."

With our bubble now popped, Kiki and I turn away from one another again. I turn in my seat to face away from both her and the mirror, not wanting to catch her eyes in the reflection. I steady my shaking hands by wiping at the globs of cream dripping down my face. Carla is as red as her bikini, sneering down at her cup as she pours herself another drink. She holds the cup out toward me, and I take it numbly despite the fact that I've barely taken a sip of my first one yet. The pain of pulling open the wound Joel left behind is too all-consuming for me to protest. There's no burn as I swallow more than half the drink in two gulps—either because gin goes down smoother, or I'm too numb to notice.

Carla clears her throat to get my attention, and I turn to find her holding something else out toward me. Another pastel-colored packet. She's wearing a smile as plastic as her acrylic nails. "For your eyes," she explains, pointing to the illustration on the side of the packet of a woman with two orbs covering her eyes. Before I can protest that I already have eyepatches on, she continues, "You'll want to close them while you have it on—this could burn the shit out of your retinas."

Behind me, I can hear Kiki stand up quickly. "Carla—"

"I'm just warning her," she snaps through her teeth before Kiki can finish, her smile too sweet. Her tone too nice. Like just one wrong move will break her.

My gut tells me to run. To find Kai and hold him close for the rest of the night. But when Carla shoots me that fake, sinister smile, I snatch the packet from her. After all the shit they've put me through tonight—all the shit people like her have put my family through the past couple of years—I won't give her the satisfaction of running away. No matter what they have in store for me tonight.

They don't scare me.

Whispers break out behind me while I apply the slimy cucumber-scented patches to my eyes. I do my best to make out the tidbits of their conversation, Kiki's voice urgent while Carla's is more casual. They must move to the opposite end of the room, their voices too muffled by the music for me to make out what they're saying. Still, I straighten my back and prepare myself for what they have in store for me. Telling my story was a much-needed reminder of everything my family has been through—everything I've survived. A stupid little prank is nothing.

If Kiki doesn't want me to date her brother, fine. If Carla hates me because of who my father is, fine. I don't need girls like Kiki or Carla to accept me as one of them, even if it means giving up Kai in the process. As good as it feels to have found someone who sees me as a person and not just a small-town mystery, it's not worth all of this. If they're not willing to see me as a person after I poured my heart out, that's their problem.

I'm done caring what other people think.

"Carla," Kiki snaps, almost a shout.

Whatever she's protesting, Carla doesn't seem to listen. She stomps across the room, so heavily I can feel the vibration even through the carpeted floor—her footsteps getting louder and louder the closer she gets to me. Before I can brace myself for what might come, something comes crashing over me. Wet and hot and putrid. It knocks the masks off my eyes and embeds itself in every part of me—my eyelashes, my mouth, my nose. Thick clumps of it drip off me, chunks of something fleshy and soft mixed into the thick, dark liquid. Something awful. Something familiar.

Blood.

21

All my senses are overwhelmed. The thick, too-warm blood drips down my cheeks to my chin and splatters onto my hands. The smell clogs my nostrils, crawling down my throat until it feels like my mouth is full of it. Some slips past my lips, staining my tongue, the taste alone making me want to retch onto the carpet. But there's nothing in my stomach to give up.

Behind me what feels like a dozen voices battle to be heard, but all of them are drowned out by the screaming. High-pitched and raw like someone's been stabbed straight through the gut. It finally cuts off when a heavy hand slaps down onto my shoulder. It's me, I realize. I was the one who was screaming.

"What the fuck did you do to her?" Kai's voice is louder than the thunder rumbling outside, the storm now at its peak. The windows rattle as the wind whips branches, leaves, and dirt through the air. Angry and raging, like I've found a way to bend nature to my own emotions.

"We di—"

"It was her," Kiki interjects before Carla can finish, her voice almost as loud and harsh as Kai's.

I blink open my eyes just enough to see Kiki pointing a

finger accusatorily at her best friend. Her eyes are narrowed to slits, her nostrils flaring like those of a bull prepared to charge. Focusing on them gives me time to try to slow my racing heart—to come down from the spike of adrenaline. There are a dozen different things I should do. Try to clean myself off, or better yet, leave while I still can, but I'm glued to the mirror as I watch Carla slowly back away from the twins until she's trapped in the corner of the room.

"I told her to stop," Kiki seethes. "I told her it was going too far."

The moments before the blood crashed onto me are a blur, but pieces begin to seep through the cracks in my memory. The look of panic on Kiki's face when Carla handed me the eye patches. The urgent hushed whispers behind me before everything went fully dark. A voice I swore shouted "no."

It seems impossible for Kiki to have sided with me on something. Especially if it meant turning against Carla. And if this had happened an hour earlier I wouldn't believe her at all. Would just assume she's trying to get out of facing the consequences of doing something she knew was wrong. But there's no denying the fury in her eyes as she glares at Carla like she's moments from lunging at her. Or the way Carla, for the first time since I've known her, looks scared shitless.

"It was just a joke," she says with a choked laugh, glancing nervously between Kai and Kiki. She crosses her arms, running her clawlike red nails along her forearms. Some of the blood must've splattered onto her. The harder she rubs her hands down her arms, the more stained they become. It doesn't take long for the blood to coat her until it looks like she's the one bleeding. When she goes to rub the back of her neck, she leaves a finger-shaped swipe down her collarbone.

"This isn't a fucking joke, Carla," Kai snaps, spit flying from his mouth and onto Carla's cheek. She winces when it makes contact, but Kai doesn't stop. "This isn't funny. It's *cruel.*"

"They killed Jose," Carla spits back, voice feral like a wounded lone wolf.

"*She* didn't do anything!" Kai shouts back so loud it makes my ears ache.

Whatever Carla does or says next to justify herself, I don't make out. Something solid falls into my lap, breaking free from being tangled somewhere in my hair. It's fleshy and cold like a piece of raw meat and is definitely the source of the smell. A wave of rot washes over me, overwhelming me until I bend over the vanity and gag.

My fingers grip the edge of the vanity for purchase as I hoist myself up. Spit clings to the edge of my lip, but nothing else comes up. Not for long, though. I can tell from the way my throat burns that my body has finally found something to throw up. Blood stains the all-white wood of the vanity as I hold onto it for balance. The stool I'd been sitting on looks as if it's been dyed—blood and clumps of whatever fell out of my hair dripping onto the plush white carpet.

I take off as fast as I can, resisting the instinct to clamp a hand around my mouth as the urge to be sick overwhelms me.

If the others notice me bolting out of the room, they don't do anything to stop me. I can vaguely hear Kai shouting at Carla, followed by Kiki chiming in immediately after him. I'm too overwhelmed by the nausea to grasp onto what they're saying, focusing all my energy on not vomiting onto the carpet. Once I'm out in the hallway, my mind goes blank. I know there's a bathroom somewhere down this hall, but can't remember which of the various closed doors lead to it. And based on the way my throat burns and my mouth starts to water, I don't have time for trial and error.

Instead, I rush down the stairs. I'm weighed down by blood, heavy like I just dunked myself in and out of the hot tub fully clothed. Still, I move as fast as I can, struggling not to slip as my soaked feet stain the sleek wood floors. Thankfully, I'm able to make it to the bathroom just in time. I slam the door behind me, bloody palm prints lining the walls and toilet seat as I collapse onto the ground and empty the contents of my stomach into the bowl.

Every part of me burns. My throat, my lips, my temples. The room rattles from thundering footsteps stomping down the stairs above me, voices shouting out in the hall, but I can't focus on anything other than getting rid of everything inside me.

"This is bullshit!" I can hear Carla shout before more footsteps come racing past the door, followed by a slam. The sliding door, most likely.

The voices don't follow Carla outside. Surrounded by silence, I focus on leveling out my breathing. Regaining control of my trembling body—first my hands, then my legs, until I can lift myself up. It takes more time than I anticipated, long enough that my joints begin to ache from staying folded around the toilet bowl. Finally, I'm able to prop myself up against the sink. The blood still coating my face and body is dried, tacky and stiff with every movement. I rub at my eyes until I can get a good look at my reflection—and instantly wish I hadn't.

Wrecked doesn't even begin to cover it. My hair is gnarled with knots, blood, and whatever those foul-smelling chunks are. It's coated on every part of me—from my eyelashes to my flannel to my chewed-up fingernails. Every inch of skin is stained deep, dark red. I look like the devil everyone's always accusing me of being.

I switch on the tap and do my best to wipe down my hands, but just like with the words painted onto our house, red is the hardest to get out. Scarlet water swirls down the drain but my skin is still stained with it—so embedded into me that it'll probably take hours to scrub it all off.

I never should've come here.

The thought hits me like an electric spark, jolting me slightly. Igniting something in me. Rage. Sadness. Fear. From the moment I stepped into their room I knew Kiki and Carla had something planned for me. That they'd do anything to scare me off. But I never could've anticipated this—any of it. Timothy and his forceful grip and wandering hands. Carla meeting my deepest pain with casual cruelty. Blood, dripping off me like water. This night was supposed to be the start of something new with me and Kai—and it was. I got the kiss I'd dared to hope for. I'll never regret what happened between us, but I do regret coming here. If it wasn't crystal clear before, it is now: All the people in this town want to do is hurt me.

What would it be like to hurt them back for once?

Like earlier with Timothy—how easy would it have been to drive a shard of glass into his neck? Or now with Carla. Just a small push or a bite to her arm—something, anything to let her feel a small piece of the pain I've dealt with over the past year.

A scream rips through the heavy silence, pulling me away from that dangerous line of thought. Guttural as I had been earlier, but louder, more desperate. I stare intently at my reflection, waiting for my lips to part to match the sound of the screams. To realize it was me all along again. But my lips don't move, and the screams don't stop.

They just get louder.

22

The screams stop the moment I burst through the door—cutting off abruptly instead of slowly fading away.

There's no sign of anyone out in the living room. It must have stopped storming while I was in the bathroom, because everything is completely silent. In the moonlit darkness, all I can make out are the bloody hand and footprints I'd left behind. I glance up at the staircase I just came from, but there's no one crumpled over or stomping their way down. Still, I can't shake the feeling that something is off. Then I realize with a gulp that the front door to the cabin is wide open.

I thought I'd heard Carla head out onto the deck, but maybe I was wrong. But if she did go through the front door, why leave it open? I approach the door slowly. The front steps are slick and slippery, but there's nothing falling from the sky except for the occasional droplet from the gutters overhead. I quickly scan for any signs of Carla from the entryway, avoiding stepping outside and risking slipping in the darkness. There's no sign of her anywhere though, so I quickly shut the door and lock it.

When I turn back around, I see it. Blood smeared on the glass of the sliding door. A sight so jarring I don't even realize I'm shaking until I attempt to head to the kitchen and stumble to my knees. Picking myself back up as quickly as I can, I grasp along the kitchen counter until I find the knife block, pull on the largest handle, and inch toward the sliding door. I may not have trusted myself with a knife earlier, but this is different. Before, I was worried about overreacting. But I've seen now how ready and willing these people are to hurt me. Now, I *know* I need protection.

Now, I'm not afraid to fight back.

It's just the animal blood, I tell myself the closer I get to the deck. *Carla must've smudged the glass when she went outside.*

When I first peek through the door, the deck looks empty. I open the slider, take a tentative step outside, and feel a familiar slippery warmth beneath my toes, different from the puddles of rain dotted around the deck.

Turns out, someone is out here.

Carla is crumpled on the ground, face upturned toward the sky. Her skin is as pale as the moonlight illuminating her, a single trail of blood trickling out of her slightly open mouth.

A thousand words sit on the tip of my tongue, but I can't choke out any of them. Not even a scream. Instead, my body moves on instinct as I drop the knife, kneel down beside her, and try to gently shake her by the shoulders.

"Carla?" I choke out when she doesn't respond to my touch, her eyes staring blankly. Her hand falls limply off where it was cradled against her chest, revealing a large gaping wound cut straight down the center of her body.

I inhale sharply, resisting the urge to be sick again. I reach for her wrist this time, gently pressing against the thin skin as I look for any sign of a pulse that I know deep down won't be there.

This can't be happening, this can't be happening, this can't be happening runs on repeat in my head, overlapping and getting louder and louder until my racing thoughts are the only thing I can hear.

This can't be happening again.

Cries for help escape me without any conscious effort, my body going into pure survival mode. We have no way to call for an ambulance. No way to turn on the lights and try to patch up the wounds ourselves. Forget waiting for Timothy—we need to leave *now*. I'm not sure if there's anything left that we can do for Carla, but the longer we stay here, the farther gone she is.

"Help!" I cry out, fingers scrambling to try to pull my phone out of my pocket—to at least give us some light to see just how badly Carla's been injured. I'm able to pry it out, but my hands are shaking too badly, my fingers too slippery from the fresh blood to grip it properly, and it goes tumbling onto the floor.

I keep shouting for help as I run my hand along the deck, looking for my phone. As soon as my fingers touch something solid they close around it without another thought, pain instantly rushing through me as I realize I grabbed the blade of the kitchen knife.

"Dammit," I mumble as I shove the knife aside, and finally find my phone.

After placing it on the ground beside me face up so I can use the light to see, I hold my injured hand against my chest. The wound isn't deep, but the pain is searing. Blinding like the worst kind of paper cut. I wince as I wrap the edge of my flannel around it, doing my best to stop the bleeding.

Thundering footsteps approach from inside the cabin. Kai and Kiki come barreling out through the sliding door together, panicked and frantic. Sweat dots Kai's brow as he rushes over to my side, glass crunching beneath his sneakers as he kneels down beside me. We never cleaned up the vase from earlier. The whole deck is still a minefield.

"Are you—"

He's cut off by Kiki letting out a high-pitched scream much like the one that led me out to the deck in the first place. She collapses beside Carla, eyes wide as she runs her hand along her blood-smeared cheeks. Her lower lip quivers, her hands trembling as she closes hers around Carla's and lifts it up toward her chest. But Kiki isn't able to maintain her grip. Carla's limp hand falls back down with a heavy, sickening *thunk*.

"You're okay, you're okay, you're okay," Kiki repeats as fast as she can, like if she says it enough times it might finally come true. She whips off her hoodie to dab at the blood on Carla's cheeks, dragging it down her collarbone and toward her chest, where she finally sees the wide-open wound. She lets out another, even louder scream.

Kai is frozen beside me, half-kneeling and shaking like a leaf as he stares wide-eyed at his sister and her dead best friend. His lips part, and in between jagged huffs of breath he lets out a series of clipped, unfinished murmurs that sound like *what happened*.

I don't know, I want to say but can't. Tears stream down my cheeks, my own arms shaking from the force of keeping myself propped up as I watch Kiki fold herself over Carla's body, wailing into the crook of her neck.

We should leave. We should run away while we still can—get in the car and drive far away from this place. But we're all frozen in place.

Slowly, Kiki hoists herself back up. She attempts to wrap her hoodie against Carla's chest as if to stop the bleeding, but her bleeding has already stopped. They're soaked in it, both of them. Kiki's hands shake so violently they're practically vibrating as she runs a hand along Carla's arm, feeling for something when she knocks against the knife I'd pushed away moments before they arrived.

Her eyes widen as she realizes what she's looking at, her sobs cutting short as she follows the trail of blood behind it.

A trail that leads directly to me.

"You," she snarls. And then I start to see what she sees: Her best friend, mauled and covered in blood. A knife with a stained blade. Me, the girl Carla just played a twisted prank on, sitting only a few feet away.

"I di—"

Kiki doesn't let me finish. In the flash of a second, she grabs the knife off the ground, holds it high above her head, and screams at the top of her lungs—coming straight for me.

23

"You fucking did this!" Kiki shouts as she lunges at me.

Kai only narrowly manages to stop her, standing up just in time to take the brunt of her weight as she barreled toward me. I press myself as far back as I can, panicking when I realize I've been backed into a corner. But even if I could run, where would I go? They know this place better than I ever will. Even in the dark.

"Kiki, stop!" Kai shouts.

With a heave, he's able to push her back toward the sliding door. Kiki flails against his hold, doing her best to wriggle away from him, but he's too strong. He grabs her wrist and tightens his grip just enough for her to let out a quiet whimper of pain and drop the knife.

My gut tells me to grab it as Kai catches the handle before it can hit the ground, and tosses it haphazardly back into the house toward the kitchen. But my brain warns me that grabbing a weapon just confirms what they think about me. They won't care that I just want to protect myself—they'll only see a murderer finishing what she started.

Finally, Kiki either gives up or runs out of energy to keep fighting. She slumps against Kai and he lets go of her wrist to wrap his arms around her. She buries her face in his neck as she sobs.

"She did it," she says between her tears. "She fucking killed Carla."

Kai looks over his shoulder at me, a desperate look on his face.

"I didn't do it," I blurt out before anyone can interrupt me, holding Kai's eyes with as much intensity as I can muster. Trying to communicate to him that I know how this looks, but that I really didn't have anything to do with it. "I think there's someone out there. I thi—"

"Don't come near me!" Kiki warns when I attempt to hoist myself up from my knees. Tears stream freely down her cheeks, cracking her picture-perfect foundation. Mascara is smudged beneath her eyes. Blood smeared along her cheeks and trembling hands.

"Let's just—"

Kiki doesn't let Kai finish. She yanks herself out of his hold, grabs his sleeve, and attempts to drag him back into the cabin. "C'mon," she commands, tugging him with all her strength. "We're getting out of here."

The thought of being stranded out here with no power, no phone service, and no way to get home makes me leap into action. I stand back up and cross the deck as quickly as I dare—narrowly avoiding stepping on glass, or worse, Carla. I make it to the sliding door in time to see Kai digging his feet into the ground until he's finally able to stop Kiki from pulling him toward the front door.

"We're not going anywhere without Dina!" he shouts before wriggling out of her hold. He freezes when he spots me in the doorway, glancing over his shoulder at Kiki before crossing back toward me, and slamming the sliding door shut.

"We're getting out of here together," he insists once we're

all locked back inside the cabin. He points to the blood staining the sliding door. "Before whoever killed Carla comes for us next."

"She's standing right there, Kai," Kiki protests, gesturing toward me. "She had a goddamn knife in her hand. Her dad's a fucking murderer!"

She stretches the last word out syllable by syllable, punctuating each one by clapping her hands together. Each clap feels like a slap across the face. But I hold my ground. She's not the first person to assume I'm a monster. But this is the only time defending myself has meant protecting my life.

"I didn't do it," I say again, even if it is pointless. My voice confident and steady, unlike hers. We already made the mistake of letting the world think Papi was guilty, but I've learned from his mistakes. I'll do anything they want if it means proving what I know to be true: that I'm innocent.

"I was in the bathroom when I heard screaming, so I got a knife from the kitchen and found Carla out on the deck. She was already . . ." Tears well up in my eyes. Every word I get out without Kiki interrupting me is precious, so I have to use them wisely. I hold up my bloodied hands, showing the gash cut through my hand. "I dropped my phone and was looking around for it, but I grabbed the knife instead when—"

"You expect me to believe that?" Kiki says with a humorless laugh. "Carla pulls some stupid prank on you and then just *happens* to end up dead? And you, the daughter of a fucking convicted killer, with a knife in your hands at the scene of the crime, had *nothing* to do with it? You're telling me I should push aaalll that aside and instead believe that someone is out there lurking in the woods picking us off for no reason?"

Her sneer causes a combination of shame and rage to

bubble inside me, quickly heating to its boiling point. My fingers clench into fists despite the gash on my right hand. I push the pain down, the way I always do. “I’m not my dad,” I say through gritted teeth.

But that doesn’t matter to Kiki. “And what about Timothy?” she continues, as if she hadn’t heard me. “What did you to do him?”

“I didn’t—”

“What did you do to them?!” she shouts loud enough to rattle the overhead light hanging above us.

“Stop!” Kai insists again, standing between me and Kiki. “Everyone just be fucking calm. I’ll get my keys and we can drive to a . . . a gas station or something and call for help.”

“Not with her.” Kiki’s eyes narrow to slits as she crosses her arms, digging her nails into the taut skin of her forearms. “I’m not going anywhere with her.”

Kai glances over at me, and I can see his resolve faltering.

“Please don’t leave me,” I beg.

My heart is lodged in my throat, threatening to make me sick for a second time as Kai looks between me and his sister. I wouldn’t blame him for running away. For putting as much distance between us as he possibly can. If I were in his shoes I’d probably run too. Who would trust a murderer’s daughter in a cabin soaked with blood?

But my foolish heart can’t help but hope that he sees the truth. That he sees the good in me, like he always has. He holds my gaze for what feels like hours—the contact only broken when Kiki attempts to tug him to the door again.

“We’re taking my car and getting out of here,” she states, pulling him the last of the way toward the front door.

But when she reaches the entryway table, she stops.

"Where the fuck are the keys?" Kiki chokes out, more to herself than to us. The bowl that once held all their keys is empty.

"I don't—"

"Where the *fuck* are the keys?!" Kiki shouts before Kai can finish, pushing him aside and heading right for me again.

Just as Kiki storms toward me, a deafeningly loud knock shakes the entire cabin. Then another, and another. Kiki stops in her tracks and Kai stumbles away from the door as the knocking gets faster and faster before stopping entirely. In a brief moment of clarity, I turn around to the sliding door and lock it—but with a door made of glass, it won't stand up very well in a fight.

And whoever is outside won't wait long to find a way in.

EXHIBIT K: FINGERPRINT ANALYSIS

A total of two sets of unique fingerprints were found on the axe collected from the scene at Albee Way, believed to be the murder weapon in the homicides of Carla Gutierrez and Timothy Gibson. The first set of fingerprints are confirmed to belong to Kai Thompson. The second, and more abundant set of fingerprints, are confirmed to belong to Dina Soto.

24

"What the fuck is that?!" Kiki shouts.

"Someone's here," Kai says, stating the obvious in an eerily calm voice.

Both of them are frozen in place, staring at the door with wide eyes and trembling hands, waiting for another knock, or a scream, or worse. But nothing comes. Whoever's at the door doesn't knock again. We all crane our necks for any sounds from the other side of the door—footsteps walking away, or maybe ragged breaths, but all I can hear is my own frantic heart.

When the silence isn't broken by our unexpected visitor, Kiki pivots and breaks it herself. "You're behind this," she whispers as she turns on her heels to face me, eyes narrowing to slits. "Who is that?"

"I-I don't—"

"Is it your dad?" she shouts loud enough that Kai flinches.

"My dad's in jail," I reply as calmly as I can.

"Then you sent someone else. One of his friends," Kiki continues, rambling until she finds an explanation that makes sense. A way to pin the blame on me.

Papi doesn't have any friends. None of us do, I think but don't say out loud. Because it doesn't matter. Nothing I say matters.

Kiki has made up her mind about who's responsible for whatever's going on here tonight and nothing's going to change that. Just like everyone else in this goddamn town. I'm guilty, no matter what.

"Kiki—" Kai's protest is cut short by more pounding at the door, this time violent enough to make the sturdy wood tremble. Both of them yelp as they back away from the door, but I'm still stuck in place.

"That's it," Kiki mutters under her breath, pulling her eyes free from the door and marching straight toward me.

I'd forgotten about the abandoned knife on the ground until Kiki picks it back up, the metal glinting as she holds it up beside her shoulder. She's not coming to attack me this time, though.

She has something else in mind.

"Kiki, what the f—"

"They won't get us if we have her," she announces before Kai can finish, reaching out to grab me by the arm.

She manages to catch me off guard, my brain still too frazzled by the chaos of the past several seconds to think to run away, and gets a vise grip around my arm. Immediately I attempt to wriggle away but there's no point. Going outside means facing whoever hurt Carla and probably Timothy. Even if I did get away from Kiki and found somewhere to hide in the cabin, she'd be able to track me down in no time.

"We can get them to give us the keys and we can get out of here," she announces to Kai as she tightens her grip on me.

At least she's not trying to plunge the knife straight through me anymore. Instead, she keeps it held beside my face like a warning. A reminder that if I try to run, I'll be the only one getting hurt. She tugs me closer to her, hooking an elbow around my neck, the knife hovering inches from my cheek.

This close, I can see how badly Kiki's hand is shaking—how wide with terror her eyes have become. When I'm pressed up against her chest, I can feel just how fast her heart is beating, a frantic rhythm pounding against my back as she holds me tight. Despite her fear, she has a firm grip. Her forearm is sturdy, the muscles taut from years of tossing girls like Carla into the air.

Kiki's so sure I'm involved with whoever's hunting us that she's willing to hold me hostage—use me as bait to lure in the killer.

The realization hits Kai later than it hits me. As soon as it does, he lunges into action.

"Have you lost your mind?" he snaps at his sister, closing the distance between us. Kiki surprises us both when she points the knife toward him instead.

"Back up, Kai," she warns, as if I'm the one who's a danger to them, as if I'm the one with the knife. "You and I are getting out of here," she whispers to him, low and menacing.

"Not like this," Kai replies, shaking his head. Then, quick as a flash, he knocks his arm against Kiki's as hard as he can.

The knife goes flying across the room. Kiki gasps, immediately letting go of me to charge after her weapon. The thought to go after the knife briefly crosses my mind, but I know that'll just wind up with someone—most likely me—getting hurt. Kai doesn't have the same line of thought, though. As soon as Kiki takes off, he follows behind her. They're evenly matched, tumbling to the floor at almost the exact same time.

I can barely make out the shapes of their bodies, but the silence is overtaken by the sounds of them fighting each other for control. A grunt from Kai. A groan from Kiki. I press myself up against the wall, doing my best to blend in with the shadows as I watch the two of them roll around the ground, the room too dark for me to properly tell them apart. I'm able to catch a glimpse of something between them—the knife gleaming as it's held in the air for a fleeting second, followed by the sound of it colliding with the ground again.

"Give it to me!" Kiki shouts, followed by a grunt that must be Kai getting hit by some part of her. "I'm keeping us safe!"

"You're making things worse!" Kai protests, the strain in his voice making it clear that they're fighting for the knife. Pushing and pulling. Impossible to tell who's in control and who's fighting to take it back.

"Just fucking—"

Whatever Kiki means to say is cut off by a *thwack* that makes the pit in my stomach rocket into my throat. I swear I hear a squelch—something wet and so stomach-churning I'm grateful I already threw up everything my body had left to give. There's a choked groan, and then silence. The worst kind of silence, broken by a whimper.

"Kiki . . ."

Kai's voice is so quiet I almost miss it. I scramble forward as quickly as I can, feeling my way through the dark toward the outlines of the twins, but I stop halfway when I realize one of the outlines isn't moving. Kiki lies flat on her back. Her eyes wide open, lips parted with nothing but a quiet, barely-there breath.

The knife sticking straight out of her chest.

25

"Dina." Kai's voice finally pulls my attention away from Kiki's body. I look up at him through the dark and can barely make out the shadow of his arm reaching toward me.

My brain tells me to run away from him, but my heart begs me to stay. To believe that he wouldn't purposefully stab his twin sister—that he wouldn't do the same to me, if I got in his way. *He did it to protect you*, I try to tell myself to calm the panic flooding through me, threatening to make me bolt out into the woods to get as far away from this place as possible. *He's not that kind of person*, I tell myself easily, but it's harder to convince myself to believe it.

Didn't I say the same thing about my family last year? And look where we are now.

Kai's arm stills when he sees me stumble back from him, falling limply to his side as he breaks out into quiet, whimpering sobs.

"I-I didn't . . . she pulled and she . . . I let go . . . I didn't . . . ," he stammers, unable to form a full sentence. "I didn't mean to," he repeats again and again, his voice a broken whisper. Confirming what I knew deep down—he would never hurt someone on purpose. Tears stream down his cheeks and blood—either his or Kiki's—travels over his wrist to stain the cuff of his shirt.

We only have a small window of time to help Kiki before she winds up like Carla. There's only so much we can do, but every second counts.

"We need to help her," I tell Kai, my own voice shaking.

"W-we don't have the keys," Kai stammers out, the tears coming even faster as it dawns on him how terrible our situation is.

"Then we have to try to help her here," I say.

I run into the kitchen and grab the paper towels I remember seeing on the edge of the counter before returning to Kiki's side. Suddenly, I wish I'd paid more attention in biology. That I knew more about the body and what it needs to survive. I have no idea if it's better to leave the knife inside of her, or if we should try to pull it out, but I can at least apply pressure. Kiki lets out a pained groan and the towels soak through almost instantly, my palms damp again from a new type of blood. It's impossible to tell how deep the wound is, but based on how little I can see of the knife's blade, I know we're working with limited time.

But how much can we do, really? It's only a matter of time until the person hunting us gets inside, through another door or a window. And when they do, we won't have anywhere to run. It's either fight or wind up like Carla.

Kai stumbles closer to me, collapsing beside his sister. His sobs have slowed, but he's trembling so badly it's a miracle he's still holding himself up at all.

"Apply pressure here," I tell him as I guide his hands toward where I've pressed a wad of the paper towels to the edge of the blade. Kiki whimpers when Kai's hands take over for mine, applying a heavier pressure.

Instantly, he drops his hands, looking down at the blood staining them in horror.

"I-I can't," he chokes out, looking from his stained hands to Kiki as she beings to writhe.

I do my best to stabilize her with a hand against her shoulder, worried the knife will go in deeper or fall out if she moves. One small mercy is she's too delirious from the pain to realize I'm the one helping her. I pick up the towels Kai dropped, holding them back in place and applying an even, steady pressure with one hand while holding down her shoulder with the other.

"I-is she gonna be okay?" Kai asks between sobs, hands trembling as he reaches out to take Kiki's in his.

In the few seconds since I pressed the paper towels against her wound, she's gone limp. Her eyes are glossy and unfocused, her breath coming out in short, sporadic bursts. It grows shallower and shallower, until the only sign I have that she's still alive is the faint rise and fall of her chest against my palms. She's still with us, but I'm not sure she will be for long.

My mind reels with a thousand questions and not a single solution, panic threatening to take over. But one of us has to stay calm if we want to make it out of here alive. If we want any chance of saving Kiki. And as much as I want to lie to Kai and tell him that everything will be fine, I can't look at him—broken and sobbing as he looks down at his dying sister—and not tell him the truth.

"I don't—"

I'm cut off by another round of pounding at the door. We both jump back, Kai toppling over onto his butt while I drop the wad of tissues. Kiki's the only one who doesn't react, her eyes finally slipping closed. Before I can panic about what that might mean, a voice calls out to us from the other side of the door.

"Dina!"

"What's going on?" Kai asks, looking frantically between me and the door as the knob begins to jiggle, followed by more pounding. It's steadier now, heavier, not from a fist or an arm or even a shoulder.

From an axe.

"Who is that?" Kai continues, grabbing my arm with an unexpected amount of force, his fingertips smeared with Kiki's blood. "Dina, who is that?!"

Fear finally takes over. Clogs my throat and steals my breath. The nagging feeling that's clung to me ever since I got here consumes me whole like the darkness.

Coming here was foolish—I've always known that. Thinking that Kai's friends would accept me even more so. But I was so desperate to take control of my life that I didn't care. It didn't matter that I was making a foolish choice so long as it was my choice to make—something I haven't done in years. Maybe ever, really. But there was a deeper fear that I'd ignored the minute I agreed to Kai's invitation. Something I told myself wouldn't happen because we'd already hit rock bottom. Things were already as horrible as they could possibly be. We were the town villains. Enemies of people who'd never met us. No chance of us ever making friends, at least not ones who knew what our family had done. Finally, we were as closed off from the world as Mami wanted us to be. There wasn't anything else to lose.

But I was wrong. It's happening—again. The same thing that ruined our lives. That put Papi away.

Mikey tried to warn me, to tell me that I was in trouble. And I was the fool who let myself believe that he was just talking about a harmless prank. When I knew just how awful things could be.

Legs shaking, I stumble up to my feet just as the axe breaks through the wood of the door. So similar to the one we buried in the backyard deep underground where we were sure the cops would never find it, hoping that they couldn't pin the murders on Papi. But you don't need a murder weapon to find someone guilty.

Through the splintered door I catch glimpses of the person on the other side. Blood-soaked hands gripping the axe's worn wooden handle, stained with mud and wet leaves and dried blood from two boys long buried. Wild brown eyes and a wolflike snarl. A glistening gold ring on her left hand—the one she refuses to take off, even though her husband is never coming back.

Somewhere behind me Kai shouts in protest as I march toward the door, but I don't hear anything he says. Don't hear anything but the pounding of my heart and my feet against the wood floor. My lungs burn from the effort of holding in a vicious scream as I throw the door open, the axe tumbling out of the wood and falling to the ground. And, finally, I'm face-to-face with the person responsible for all of it. For ruining my life. Joel's. For taking someone else's—those boys'. Carla's. Papi's. Whose smile I inherited. Vicious and full of sharp teeth. I tried running away from her, but I should've known she'd find a way to track me down.

Mami was never going to let me leave.

26

"How did you find me?" I spit at Mami through gritted teeth, my nails digging into my blood-tacky palms.

Looking at her—braid matted by rain and blood splattered across her hands, arms, face—it's impossible not to remember that night. How wild she looked when she came storming into the house, ordering for Papi to grab a shovel from the backyard shed to help her dig. The way she ignored all of my and Mikey's questions and told us to stay in our rooms. The unease in my stomach as we watched from my bedroom window as Papi and Mami dug a hole so deep it came nearly to their shoulders, tossing an axe that had been collecting dust in the shed into it. The same one Papi had warned us a dozen times never to touch.

It's not the same axe in her hands now, though it's so covered in mud you might think it was. It took her and Papi hours to dig a hole deep enough to hide the proof of what she'd done—she wouldn't have wasted that kind of time tonight. Instead, the perfect weapon was sitting in the driveway, as if it was waiting for her to take it.

"They hurt you," Mami spits back, ignoring my question, her voice rough and gravelly as stone. She's heaving for breath from the effort of driving the axe through the door. From what she did to Carla and Timothy.

She killed them. Just like she killed those boys. Even after she said it was an accident. Even after she promised she wouldn't do it again. Even after Papi gave up everything to save her.

"They didn't—"

"I saw them!" Mami shouts before I can finish. "That girl and her boyfriend. Laughing like hyenas at the Costco. Calling their friends and telling them they were going to pull a *Carrie* on some girl. When I realized you were missing, that's when I knew it was meant for you."

"How did you find me?" I whisper again, struggling to keep my voice even, knowing that there's only one way she could've found out where I'd gone. And I wouldn't put it past her to hurt him too. "What did you do to Mikey?"

She scoffs. "Nothing. He told me where you went, and I told him to stay home," she spits back, seemingly offended at my implication. "I would never hurt either of you." She holds her hand against her heart, eyes softening for a fraction of a second, but I don't let that brief slip change my mind.

Because it's not true. She hurts us every day. Has for years. The strict rules. The curfews. Punishing us for trying to find a life outside of the confines of our house. Making sure she was the only person we could ever trust. Just because she's never laid a hand on us, doesn't mean she hasn't hurt us in ways that have irrevocably shaped us.

"It was just a stupid prank," I mutter, not as strong as I'd like to be. The thought of Carla and Timothy bragging about their plans for me stings, but nothing hurts as badly as knowing that they're gone because of me. I didn't deserve their wrath, but they didn't deserve hers either.

"You don't even know these people," Mami continues, completely ignoring what I just said. As usual. It's always been about what she thinks. What she believes. She hasn't listened to us—any of us—for years. Maybe not ever. "Or that boy." She points her finger at where Kai is trembling over my shoulder, frozen in place from the shock of what he's witnessing.

"Don't," I shout. I can only hold back my rage for so long—the anger bubbling inside of me, simmering hotter and hotter with every passing second. Burning brighter with every new horrifying detail I discover on her: Blood staining her gloved hands. Claw marks etched across her cheek. One of Carla's ruby red nails clinging to the ends of Mami's braid.

I step directly between her view of Kai, shielding him from her. For now, at least.

"He's my friend," I say, the words so low they're practically a growl.

Mami lets out a cold, humorless bark of a laugh, shaking her head like I'm some naive little kid. "These aren't your friends."

She's right, but I'd never admit it. Especially not now when she could use it as justification for the twisted crusade she's on.

"Where's Timothy?" I ask, refusing to let her think she has the upper hand here.

"He looked at you like you were an animal," she says with a snarl, tightening her grip on the axe's handle, her leather gloves squelching in a way that makes me sick. "Like something he wanted to tame. And he wouldn't even own up to it when I told him to apologize for what he did to you."

Timothy wasn't just wandering around in the middle of a storm. *She* found him. The thought of the two of them going head-to-head in the middle of the woods makes me sick. She's the reason he didn't come back. I thought Timothy was the only thing I had to be afraid of out here, but I was so, so wrong.

"He got what he deserved," Mami says through gritted teeth.

"None of them *deserve* this." I don't realize I'm crying until I feel the warmth of the tears slipping down my cheeks—hear the tremble in my voice. The image of Mami begins to blur as I give myself over to the pain. The sadness. Reality weighs a thousand tons as it slowly settles over me.

Mami has always held us close. Too close. Both before Joel and after we lost him. Hurt from her own childhood bled into ours, made her fear what the world would do to us to the point where she became the very thing she was trying to protect us from.

Our already tight leash only got shorter when we lost Papi—when he took the fall for her. We were all being punished for what *she* did. None of what happened was ever fair, but that was one part I could never understand. Why were we held tighter when *she* was the one who hurt someone, who hurt us? This time, the outside world wasn't to blame—she was.

Despite all her efforts, it's not the world I'm afraid of. I'm not afraid of Kai or Kiki or Carla, even after they were cruel to me. I'm not even afraid of Timothy. The thing I'm most afraid of is *her*.

I knew when I saw the blood on her hands that night a year ago that our lives would never be the same. Our nightmare had just begun. And now here we are, living it out again.

"They hurt you!" Mami repeats, a shout this time, and I can tell from the way her voice cracks that she does it through tears. But I don't have the same sympathy for her now that I had then, so soon after we lost Joel. When she spent all her nights curled up in a messy bed he'd never make again. When she buried her face in his pillow until all she could smell was herself.

Papi told me to go easy on her. Her grief was all-consuming, she didn't know what she was doing, wasn't in her right mind. She was already suffering so much—but why did that give her the right to make us suffer, too?

"That doesn't mean they should die!" I yell back, resisting the urge to push her.

Papi said he would take the blame because he was stronger. Because Mami only did what she did because the world kept letting her down. First, her mother, who would sooner punish her than show her any kind of love. Then, her school. For not seeing the way the other kids tortured her or the marks her mom left on her body. Then, the police. Failing to do anything about those boys who tortured Joel the same way her classmates had done to her all those years ago. My mother has been through a lot. But that doesn't mean she's blameless.

Looking at her now, covered in multiple people's blood, carrying the same type of weapon that she's used twice now to take four lives, I realize I hate her. I've hated her for months. Longer. A feeling that blossomed when we first lost Joel and bloomed into full-on hatred when the judge sentenced Papi to life. I didn't want to face it then. Maybe because she was all I had left. Maybe because I was afraid of not having a mother or a father. Maybe because I was afraid of what it meant to lash out against the one person who claimed she loved me more than anything—to pull apart everything I've been raised to believe piece by piece. But I'm able to embrace that feeling fully now, can feel it rushing through me until it consumes every part of me. She ruined everything—our lives, our reputations, any hope we had of being normal kids in this too-small town. She took everything I loved away from me and still has the nerve to stand here and try to take more. Until she's the only thing left.

For the first time since he agreed to take the fall for her, I'm angry at Papi too. Hate him just as much as I hate her. Because if he had let the police find out the truth—take Mami instead of him—we wouldn't be here right now. Carla. Timothy. They'd both still be alive.

She wouldn't have been able to hurt anyone else.

"You have no idea what they could've done to you!" Mami screams at me, gesturing toward the deck—where Carla's lifeless body is still slumped on the ground, where we last saw Timothy before he disappeared into the dark. "That boy touched you even though you told him no. And that girl. All those things she said about you. How she treated you like you were subhuman during that game. And now . . ." Mami glares at me with enough disdain it would make my knees tremble if I cared what she thought anymore. "Look at what they did to you."

I know how I must seem to her. Bloody and bruised. But I'm not broken—not because of them, at least. They can knock me down as many times as they want, pour as much animal blood on me as they can, but it'll never hurt the way Mami has hurt me. Not when she's the reason they wanted to hurt me in the first place.

The person standing on the doorstep isn't the same person who braided my hair growing up. Who used to watch telenovelas with me in the living room on rainy nights. That person has been gone for years—ever since Joel started high school and she realized the world hadn't gotten any kinder since she was our age. People were still as cruel as she remembered. So, she kept us close. Held us so tight it made us want to burst.

"Dina—"

“Get away from her!” Mami shouts before Kai can step toward me, wielding the axe high in the air like she’s preparing to strike.

Before she can lunge, I attack first. Tackling her from the side while her wild, feral gaze is fixed on Kai. It catches her off guard enough to throw her off balance—but not enough for her to let go of the axe. Immediately, I reach for it. Gripping the middle of the wooden handle and pulling it toward me with as much strength as I have left. For a half a second, I think I’ve pulled it free—some of the tension giving way long enough that I tip back slightly, but she yanks it back just as quickly as she let go.

We let out quiet grunts and shouts as we play our high-stakes game of tug-of-war, side-stepping through the room like a waltz as we struggle for dominance. My arms ache in protest, my body begging me to finally rest after spending the entire night feeling like I was balancing on a tightrope. The rotten smell of animal blood still stings my nose when I inhale sharply, but it only makes me pull harder. A reminder that there’s more than just store-bought blood on my hands.

With a scream and a heave, Mami lands a kick against my shin moments before tugging the axe toward her. Pain explodes down my leg, making my knees buckle as I let out a yelp. My heart rockets into my throat, my brain scrambling for a way to regain my balance, but the struggle isn’t over yet. A new hand appears beside mine, a steady, sure warmth beside me.

Kai.

Mami lets out a growl-like sound at the sight of him—of us side by side, using our combined strength to tug the handle toward us. Together, we’re strong enough to drag the axe to the tip of her fingers, her eyes narrowed to slits and her teeth bared as she snarls at us like a rabid wolf.

It all happens in a matter of seconds. Mami whipping her grip quickly to the left instead of toward her chest. Kai and I stumbling at the unexpected movement. His head colliding with the edge of the staircase banister—a sickening thud echoing through the room. Mami's cruel, cold laugh as Kai collapses at my feet. His eyes closed, his skin paling more and more by the second.

Kai was my small piece of the world that filled me with joy. A sliver of hope that I could have a normal life again someday. With someone who didn't see me as the monster everyone else decided I was. My one precious thing. My only piece of hope.

Now, she's taken that too.

27

"What did you do?" I say it quietly at first, barely a whisper. "What did you do?!" This time, it's a roar. Jagged and clawing its way out of my throat as I whip around to look at Mami with so much rage I hope it melts her on the spot.

But she doesn't fade away. She staggers up to her full height as she holds the axe against her chest—free of our meddling hands. Her hair has come loose from its braid, flyaway curls dangling in front of her face. Sweat dotting her brow. Her lips curled into a frown. We look so much alike it makes me sick.

Kai's voice on the drive up comes back to haunt me. How gutted I felt when he told me that I looked like Mami. Maybe that's why I've always loved when people tell me I look more like Papi than her—crave it, almost. A quiet confirmation that I'm not like her. I'll *never* be anything like her.

She turns slowly toward me, still heaving for breath. "I protected you."

"This isn't protecting me," I spit back. "None of this is about me."

The same way it's never been about Joel. About keeping us safe. Not really. Because if she ever stopped to think about what she was doing, she'd know we're not her. That even if the story might look the same, we're our own people. We can make our own choices, fight our own battles. Holding us close will never save us, no matter how much she thinks it will. And doing this—hurting innocent people like Kai—won't do anything to change our fate.

All it's ever done is ruin what we already have.

"He's a good person," I say through the tears falling fast and hard down my cheeks. My entire body trembles as I force myself to look at Mami head-on instead of letting my attention linger back to Kai, to where he's crumpled on the floor. Because if I look back at him and don't see his chest rising and falling with each breath, I'm not sure what I'll do.

The only thing I have left now is hope. That I'll make Mami understand. That she'll leave us alone. That we can still make it out of here alive.

"And even if he wasn't, you don't get to decide who deserves to live or die," I explain, waving my arm to where his sister is splayed across the floor, still bleeding out and unmoving. "Why can't you understand that?"

I'm not sure how loud I have to shout to make her hear me, but I say it loud enough to make her wince and step back slightly. Rage courses through me—more powerful than any adrenaline rush—as I take a step toward her. Because I'm not afraid of her anymore. Even with an axe in her hands, smeared with the blood of my classmates. I've wasted enough time living in fear of her, of what she might do if I decided to take control of my life, if I ever came clean about what she did.

I'm done being afraid. Of people like Kiki and Carla and Timothy. Of the world. But especially of Mami.

"You have to stop," I whisper to her, doing my best to keep my voice as calm and controlled as I can. My chest burns from the urge to shout at her until she finally listens. But I know shouting isn't the answer. There was plenty of that the night she killed those boys. Her, mostly. Screaming at Papi that this was what she had to do to protect our family. Because the school administration wasn't going to do anything. And the cops did even less. As if getting rid of them would bring Joel back. It was the same excuses she hurled at me now. *They hurt him.* But back then we were naive enough to think this was a onetime thing. The worst kind of lapse in judgment.

For a foolish second, I hold my breath and hope that Mami will see my side of things. Finally understand what she's put us all through and come clean to the authorities. Let Papi come home. Try to get the help she needs. Instead, the wrinkles along her brow deepen as she narrows her eyes at me. Her grip on the axe tightens as she closes the distance between us—until I can smell her evening tea on her breath.

"All I've ever wanted was to keep you safe. The way my mother never did," she says, the softness of her voice not matching the darkness in her eyes. She's glaring at me like she wishes she could cut right through me. If I close my eyes, I might be able to believe she's still the person that lives in my memories—who braided my hair with tender hands instead of tugging and pulling and rushing to get it done before running out the door. But that doesn't last long. "And you've never even cared," she sneers, the words and her tone finally matching the harshness of her body. "You've never known how horrible life can be when your mother doesn't love you. You've never understood. Never appreciated everything I've done for you. Never understood how much I *love* you."

"If this is what love is," I reply, voice steadier than it's been all night, gesturing to Kai's and Kiki's passed-out bodies, "then I don't want it."

I brace myself, prepared for her to swing the axe at me. But instead she lets go of it entirely, letting it fall to the ground with a clatter that feels louder than a thousand thunderstorms. I resist the urge to lunge for it, not sure if this is all part of some kind of plan.

Mami backs away slowly. One step, then two. Until she's nearly back at the door to the cabin. "How many times do I have to warn you before you listen? How many times do I have to watch you and your siblings get hurt before you understand that these people don't care about you? All they'll ever want is to tear you apart."

I don't protest, even though I want to. Mami's made it to the entrance now, her hand closed so tight around the doorknob that her knuckles are pale as snow. "All I've done since the day you were born is try to keep you safe," she spits out, sounding as if she regrets it now. Protecting me. "You think you don't need me? Fine." She lets out a humorless laugh before wiping away a stray tear—accidentally smearing blood along the apple of her cheek. "See how long you make it without me."

She kicks off her bloodstained shoes so roughly they fly across the room. Then she steps out of the cabin entirely and slams the door behind her. Loud enough to make me let out a quiet gasp of surprise. I'm ready for her to come barreling back into the room, swinging at me and promising to make me pay for my selfishness, but the room stays silent. The axe stays on the ground. The bodies around me don't move.

All that's left is me and the consequences of everything Mami's done.

EXHIBIT L: PHONE CALL MADE AT 11:42 p.m. ON OCTOBER 31 – EMILIA SOTO TO MILLCREEK PD

MPD: 911, what's your emergency?

ES: My daughter, she . . . She went away with some friends for the weekend, and I haven't heard from her. I've been texting and calling, but she hasn't responded. It's not like her . . .

MPD: How long has she gone without contact?

ES: About six hours.

MPD: And do you have any reason to suspect that something might be wrong?

ES: She sounded nervous. Before she left. I don't know these kids she's with and I'm just worried that they . . . I'd feel better if someone could check in on them. Make sure they're all right.

MPD: We can send an officer by if you think there might be underage drinking involved, but we can't do much else besides that, ma'am.

ES: They're definitely drinking. I saw the bottles in her bag.

MPD: All right. Do you have an address?

ES: 127 North Albee Way.

MPD: All right. We'll send an officer to check things out.

ES: Thank you . . . thank you.

28

If I thought the quiet was unsettling before, it's nothing compared to the silence after Mami leaves.

As soon as the door closes behind her I focus all my attention on Kai. Grab my phone with shaking hands and try to shine as much light on him as I can to see if he's bleeding. There are no open wounds from what I can tell, but he must've hit the banister hard enough to make him pass out. I'm not sure how long it'll last, and whether the hit to his head could have more severe consequences, but I do my best to wake him. Shake his shoulders, cry out his name, apply pressure to his chest. Every remedy I can think of to make his shallow breath come faster. But nothing changes.

Across the room, Kiki's breath is so quiet I can barely hear it even when I press myself as close to her as I dare. Both of them are running on borrowed time.

I search the cabin for the missing car keys. Open cabinets and drawers and look between sofa cushions for anything that can help get us out of here. It doesn't hit me until I've pulled out all the couch cushions that they may not just be missing, but taken. I suddenly remember the wide-open front door when I came downstairs. Mami had been in the house. She took the keys because she knew we would try to run.

This isn't like last time. When Mami lashed out at those boys, it was the heat of the moment. A case of temporary insanity. She was overwhelmed by her grief and being let down again and again and again by the systems that should've protected her. Should've protected Joel. But tonight, she thought this through. She waited outside and watched us like we were her prey. Waited until the others made their move to lash out. Waited to pick everyone off, one by one. Had she known from the minute she heard what Carla was planning that she was going to kill her? Or did she know as soon as she saw that axe in the driveway?

She had to, I realize as I stand alone in the dead-quiet living room. She could have just come and taken me home. Embarrassed me in front of everyone and grounded me for the rest of the year. But there was never any knock at the door. No calling of my name, even when I was in trouble. She never even stopped to consider that she didn't have to hurt them to save me.

At first, when I hear the crunch of something on the dirt road and the snapping of twigs, I assume Mami is back. Either to finish me, or to take me home, and I don't want to find out which.

"Kai, come on," I whisper to him, trying to get him to wake up again. I loop my arm through his, trying to hoist him up onto his feet, hoping the movement will jostle him awake.

If we can hide somewhere in the cabin, maybe she'll turn back around. Give up on the search. But Kai doesn't wake up, and moving him is harder than I thought. Light as he might be, he weighs a whole lot more when he's nothing but dead weight. I've barely even managed to get him into a sitting position when I hear a voice call out.

"Hello?"

A deep, gruff voice. A stranger. The stairs up to the cabin creak under his weight as he approaches, light from a flashlight flooding the living room as he steps up to the cracked wood of the door, fiddling with the knob for just a few seconds before it flies open. I flinch at the sudden brightness but don't let go of Kai to shield my eyes.

"Hel—"

The stranger cuts himself off with a gasp, the light stuttering as he drops his flashlight to the ground.

I realize then what he must see. Me, covered in blood, moving an unconscious body. Another person bleeding out on the floor. And the axe Mami left behind.

"I didn't do it," I blurt out, my gut speaking before my brain can catch up to it.

"Wh-what?" the man stammers out, finally finding his flashlight again and shining it directly at me. I let go of Kai to shield myself from the light this time, examining the man when he shifts the light slightly to my left once he sees me wince. Khaki pants and a shirt. A gold badge pinned to his chest. The same uniform the cops wore when they came to take away Papi.

"I didn't do it," I repeat, more confident this time. Because I won't let them take away the wrong person. Not again.

29

I'm not a stranger to guilt. I've felt an ocean's worth of it since we lost Joel. Twice that since Mami killed those boys and Papi offered himself up a few months later. A thousand what-ifs are constantly swirling around in my brain. What if I had been a better sister to Joel, made him feel at home in a house that always felt cold to him. Reminded him that we could leave someday, even if Mami told us we couldn't. What if I'd told someone the truth about what Mami did. What if I saw the signs—that she was the monster lurking in the woods outside the cabin—instead of just ignoring them.

I can't change the past, but that doesn't stop it from haunting me. Sleep has never come easy, but it was basically impossible in the days after the police found me in the cabin, curled around Kai's body. It felt like both seconds and years had passed since Mami closed the door behind her. Since she left me to the wolves.

The cop didn't believe my story at first, and I can't blame him for that. A girl with my past surrounded by bloody bodies? The headline writes itself. And it did—our names dominated the news all over again.

With Kai and Kiki out cold, I was convinced there was no way anyone would believe me. Mami would get exactly what she wanted. Just like she did last time. All that first responder could do was rush to get me locked into a cell, as far away from more people to hurt as he could. No one listened when I told them it wasn't me. No one even asked me for the truth—about what really happened. They just wanted to know how I did it. How I'd managed to take down so many people all on my own. How I got my hands on the axe. Whether I had something to do with those boys' murders last year.

The only reason they listened was because I wouldn't stop telling them. Over and over for hours repeating the exact same thing.

That I didn't do it.

None of them believed me. Who would have? The girl covered in blood trying to blame two murders on a woman who supposedly wasn't anywhere near the crime scene. I begged them to go to my house to see for themselves. Surely there'd be proof there. Something to point their attention toward Mami.

But it turns out all I needed was a witness.

The cops weren't sure what to do with me after Kai woke up and gave his testimony. He backed up my entire story, every detail matching up even though we hadn't seen each other since that night. Finally, they went to our house. They took Mikey away and asked him what he knew. He broke down. Told them the truth—that he was afraid of what Mami would do if he came forward about what she'd done. Another person proclaiming my innocence.

Mikey's gone now. Somewhere far from this town with a family that was kind enough to open their home to him until things are settled. Cops won't tell me where, insisting that it's protocol to keep us apart until after the trial. Neither of us—me or Mami—will be allowed to see him until all of this is over.

Once they decide once and for all which one of us is telling the truth.

The guilt would be enough to crush someone who wasn't already so used to carrying this much on their shoulders. Worse than the feeling of dread—of knowing I could've tried to stop this before it got out of hand—is the relief. That, deep down, no matter how hard I try to ignore it, a part of me is breathing easier knowing I don't have to go home to Mami anymore. I'd gladly spend years in a cell as long as it meant I didn't have to smile in her face and act like nothing was wrong.

Every time I linger on that feeling I shy away as if just the thought of it burns. Two more people are dead. Timothy and Carla are never coming back. I'm still not sure what happened to Kiki. With the cops refusing to declare me innocent, they're keeping me at a juvenile detention center forty-five minutes away from Millcreek. Doesn't matter that two people have agreed that I didn't do anything wrong except let Mami intimidate me into silence—they've decided I'm guilty until proven innocent.

I've seen flashes of Carla's and Timothy's parents on the TVs at the center. Timothy's mom in tears calling for our family to burn and Carla's abuela staring blankly into the distance, too stunned to say anything at all. It's the most horrifying sense of déjà vu. Except, this time, the spotlight isn't on Papi. It's on me.

The police have kept the full truth a secret. Once it came out that Mami was arrested too, the coverage escalated to a whole new level. Bigger even than Papi's trial. The murderous Soto family—not just one monster, but three. Part of me is glad that they didn't let me go home, and that Mikey is far away from here. They've even taken precautions to keep me apart from the rest of the kids at the center. At least I can ride this out alone. Until I've proven my innocence and can finally put this nightmare behind me.

Today, though, I'm not alone.

Mary, the defense attorney assigned to my case, told me that my visit today would be completely monitored. She'd be standing just a few feet away, listening to everything we say. Making sure we don't discuss details that could mess with the case. But all those rules and stipulations went in one ear and out the other because none of it mattered. All I cared about was getting to see him again.

It's jarring, being on the other side of a familiar table. There's no plexiglass separating me from the other end of the room or rundown phones we'll have to talk through, but the effect is the same. My breath hitches as I'm guided by a fleet of guards to the seat opposite Kai, Mary lingering in the corner as promised, waiting to interject. During all those visits with Papi, I never considered what it might be like to sit in his place.

I never thought I would be.

Looking him over, I realize all at once that the Kai I know might be gone. I may never get to hear that laugh, see that smile, ever again. My throat tightens as Mary goes over the rules yet again, warning us that we shouldn't discuss details about what happened that night two weeks ago. We both nod in agreement, but I'm not sure if either of us really listens. Kai's eyes stay fixed on mine the entire time—his face unchanged except for a half-healed bruise on his forehead and a cut through his lower lip.

No one would blame him if he never wanted to see me again. If he hadn't invited me into his inner circle, Timothy and Carla would still be alive. He wouldn't have to live with the trauma of knowing he accidentally stabbed his sister.

When Mary finishes her spiel and returns to her seat in the corner of the room, I half expect Kai to shout at me. I've braced myself for him to finally turn his back on me like the rest of the world did, and now's the perfect moment. One last chance to yell at me for what I put him through. What I put all of them through. To confess that he was wrong—that he was the only person who thought I wasn't a monster, when I was all along. But he doesn't say anything.

"I—"

Kai doesn't let me finish that thought. He's up and leaning across the table in the blink of an eye, and my heart races as I wonder if he's going to attack me or push me away. Instead, he's pulling me closer. His arms wrapped around my shoulders, holding me tight against his chest. His nose buried in the crook of my neck, like he's trying to inhale the scent of me.

"No touching!" Mary shouts, a new rule she'd apparently forgotten to mention. Kai doesn't pull away when she warns us, though.

"You're okay," he whispers like he can't believe it. His voice wavers, tears staining my neck as he grips me even tighter once I wrap my arms back around him. It's the safest I've felt in a long time. No lurking shadows. No lingering eyes. Just us. Just *him*.

Mary warns us again and we finally break apart, not wanting to risk getting separated seconds after we were reunited. I sit on my hands to keep them from reaching across the table for him.

"*You're* okay," I echo once we're sitting back down.

"How're you feeling?" he whispers, his own hands twitching where they're sitting in the middle of the table.

I fight back a humorless laugh, giving him a wry smile. "Shouldn't I be asking you that?"

From what Mary's told me, his injuries weren't as severe as they'd seemed that night. A concussion that he's past the worst of. A couple of bruises and sprains but nothing with lasting consequences. Unlike his sister, he made it through mostly unscathed.

"M'fine." He shrugs and rubs along the back of his neck, the smooth, sharp lines of his fresh undercut now faded. "Mainly just been sitting around at home until I have the all clear to go back to school."

"Is Kiki okay?" I ask quickly, wringing my fingers together to keep my nerves at bay. If anyone is going to be honest with me about how she's really doing, it'll be him.

"She will be," he says with a tight smile, his eyes glazed and distant, as if he's trying to fight back tears. "It was pretty touch and go for the first few days, but she's stable now. Gonna need a shitload of physical therapy, and she probably won't be able to stay on the cheerleading squad, which'll piss her off. But stable."

Some of the tension in my chest eases, but doesn't fully relax. I don't know if it ever will—knowing how much was taken away from Kiki because of me. My throat tightens at the thought of how angry she must be. How much Kai must regret inviting me to their cabin in the first place. I can promise him a thousand times that I didn't know Mami was lurking in the woods, that I genuinely didn't think she was capable of doing this again, but that doesn't change what happened.

"Kai, I'm so sor—"

"Did you know?" he interrupts before I can run through the apology I've had nothing but time to rehearse. His expression is unreadable. "About your mom?"

I shake my head so quickly it makes the world spin, my thoughts rattling around my brain like a pinball machine. "I had no idea that she followed me that night, I swear," I promise him with all the strength and conviction I have left to give. "I didn't realize it was her until after we found Carla, and—"

"I meant . . ." He trails off after cutting me short, looking down at his scuffed sneakers. Avoiding my eyes. "About before. What she did to those other guys."

I swallow hard, even though I knew the question was coming. How could it not be, when it's been splashed all over the news for weeks? *Daughter of infamous convicted killer accuses her mother of four murders.* No matter how many times I prepared myself to tell him the truth, I still feel unsettled by the prospect of it. I've told my story dozens of times over the past two weeks. To detectives and lawyers and reporters. This is different, though. "Yes."

He bites his lip, peeking up at me from beneath his full lashes. "And you didn't tell anyone?"

Dozens of excuses sit on the tip of my tongue. *Because I thought she wouldn't do it again. Because Papi told me not to. Because I thought it was safer not to. Because I wasn't sure anyone would believe me if I did.* "Because I was afraid," I say finally, after several seconds of silence. The truth. The ugly, selfish, undeniable truth. If I had just been a little braver, a little bolder, a little smarter, maybe I could've saved Carla and Timothy. I definitely could've saved me and Mikey a whole lot of grief. Mami's greatest talent was making sure we were driven by fear. It's what kept us close to home. Ultimately, it's what kept us quiet too.

Where would we be if I'd just had the strength to be honest?

"If I'd known this would happen, I would've told someone in a heartbeat but . . ." I'm not sure how to finish that statement, so I don't. I force myself to look Kai in the eyes as I confess to yet another dark truth nestled deep inside of me. "Now all I can do is regret it. For the rest of my life."

No matter how this turns out—if I'm locked away forever or if Mami is—I can't change what's already happened. Even if things change for the better—if Papi and Mikey finally get to come home, if we get a second chance to rebuild our lives together—we'll always be haunted by our pasts. Justice will never be enough.

"People keep asking me how I feel about you. After everything . . ." he says, his eyes falling to the ground, and my heart rockets into my throat. "If I hate you for being . . . tied to her."

I fully expect him to pull back from me. Who would blame him? I'm still the murderer's daughter. And to some, I'm the reason two more people are dead. If it wasn't for me sneaking out, Timothy and Carla would still be alive. That guilt is something I'll never be able to shake off, but I've at least learned not to care what other people think of me. I haven't stopped caring about Kai, though. Or worrying about how he sees me.

But Kai doesn't shy away from me. The way he looks at me is still soft and tender. Like nothing has changed between us. "Those people weren't there, though. Didn't hear all those awful things your mom said. Didn't see how hard you tried to save me. And Kiki." He looks as if he's going to lean across the table to try to take my hand, but glances over at Mary and decides against risking it. "You're nothing like her," he whispers instead. "No matter what anyone says."

Even now, after everything that's happened, Kai still knows how to say the exact right thing to make my heart swell. The moment is bittersweet, though. The guilt too present for me to feel the full relief of Kai's forgiveness, his assurance I'm not like Mami. Tears cloud my vision, my hands trembling where they're clasped in front of me on the table. I look down just in time for the tears to splatter onto the table. "But I could've saved everyone."

Mary shoots me a warning look. We've delved too close to what happened that night. I don't have enough fight left to push off the guilt, so I give myself over to it. My whole body shakes from the force of my sobs as I hold my fists against my eyes, doing what I can to stop the tears, but I've learned the hard way that once they start they don't stop easily.

A warmth flows through me as a hand reaches across the table to take mine—Kai, I realize when the familiar smell of him cuts through the fog of tears and snot and sobs. "I'm so, so sorry," he whispers as he squeezes my hand. Mary looks as though she's going to protest, but ultimately decides against it.

I want to tell him that he doesn't have to apologize. How could he have known about my best kept secret? The only one who should be sorry is me, and I'll say it a thousand times and then a thousand more if it means he might believe me.

Once my sobs have subsided Kai delicately pulls back, but doesn't let go of my hand, keeping our fingers linked at the center of the table. "Do you think you'll get out of here soon?"

I shrug and sniffle as I wipe my damp cheeks. "I'm not sure."

Nothing about my future is clear. If or when I get home. What'll happen to Papi if the jury is convinced I'm telling the truth. Who Mikey and I will live with if I'm let out of here. Best-case scenario, a jury sees the mountain of evidence against Mami and believes my testimony is the truth. Worst-case scenario, Millcreek gets another juicy tabloid story about the girl who followed in her father's killer footsteps. I try not to dwell on the thought of it. Everything about our future is out of my control. I can't predict how a jury will see me—whether they'll believe anything I say or decide I'm a liar looking for revenge against a controlling mother. But at least there's small comfort in knowing some people believe me. Mary. Mikey. Kai. People who matter.

Kai brushes his thumb across the back of my hand. A simple gesture that still makes my skin ignite beneath his touch. "Are you okay?"

I shrug again, skin still prickling from the brief contact. "I'm . . ." I'm a dozen things and nothing all at once. Angry and guilty and exhausted. I've spent enough time dwelling on those thoughts, though. It only feels right to focus on the good when I'm here with Kai—who, for so long, was my one good thing. "Hopeful," I finally say, and something loosens in the pit of my stomach. A small chunk of the worry chipped away.

Kai snorts in a way that lights up the room almost as much as his smile. "Someone has to be."

I can't help but laugh, even though it's not quite genuine, only about thirty percent of me behind it. "Look on the bright side," he says with a hint of a smile as his thumb brushes along my knuckles this time. "Our next weekend trip can't possibly be any worse than this one was."

This time, nothing about my laugh is forced. The sensation is unfamiliar, like riding a bike for the first time in years, but it's like the opening of a dam. It releases something inside me that's been begging to be set free. I laugh so hard it makes him laugh too. Until we're laughing harder than the joke called for. And maybe that's wrong—to make a joke about something as horrible as what we went through together. But as I wipe at the tears in the corners of my eyes—from joy, instead of pain, for once—I can't find it in me to care. I'm too relieved to be anything but happy. Relieved that I'm still capable of laughter after everything that's happened. Relieved that Kai didn't lash out—that there's even the possibility of a next time when it comes to me and him. Relieved that, maybe, I can still have the life I never thought I deserved.

Because I'm not letting anyone make me out to be a monster ever again. Not the public, not the headlines, and definitely not Mami. I've spent enough of my life letting other people decide what I deserve. I deserve joy. I deserve laughter. I deserve *this*. All of it, with a boy who deserves them too.

ACKNOWLEDGMENTS

This book has evolved so much over the years I've spent writing it, but what's never changed is its roots. This has always been inspired by games like *Until Dawn*, and all the slasher movies I watched at three a.m. during sleepovers at my cousin's house. If you find comfort in stories that take place in the dark, this one's for you.

One thousand thank-yous to Alex Borbolla, editor extraordinaire, who helped shape Dina into the fierce, resilient Final Girl she was always meant to be!

All my gratitude goes out to the Bloomsbury team that has helped bring my darker stories into the world, including Emani Glee, Brianna Williams, and Oona Patrick. Thank you to Molly Von Borstel at Faceout Studio and Jeanette Levy for creating this gorgeous cover!

Thank you to my incredible agent, Uwe Stender, for helping me turn my childhood dream of being an author into a reality!

There's never a moment when I'm not grateful for how supportive my family has been of this journey. Thank you to Mami, Abuela, my cousins, titis, tios, madrinas, padrinos, and in-laws for coming out to all my events, sending me pictures of my books in the wild, and for believing in this dream as fiercely as I did.

Special shout-out to the amazing friends who help me unwind between writing sessions with movies and mahjong and dance class and a dozen other adventures. Y'all are the only reason I don't fall down a dark rabbit hole every time I write a thriller.

And last, but never least, Duncan. My best friend, my thesaurus, and, by the time you're reading this, my husband. :)